WEREWOLF NOEL

Big City Lycans
Book Six

New York Times and USA Today Bestselling Author

Eve Langlais

Copyright Werewolf Noel © Eve Langlais 2022/2023

Cover Art © by Melony Paradise of ParadiseCoverDesign.com 2022

Produced in Canada

Published by Eve Langlais

http://www.EveLanglais.com

eBook: ISBN: 978 1 77 384 391 9

Print ISBN: 978 1 77 384 392 6

ALL RIGHTS RESERVED

This book is a work of fiction and the characters, events and dialogue found within the story are of the author's imagination and are not to be construed as real. Any resemblance to actual events or persons, either living or deceased, is completely coincidental.

No part of this book may be reproduced or shared in any form or by any means, electronic or mechanical, including but not limited to digital copying, file sharing, audio recording, email and printing without permission in writing from the author.

PROLOGUE

It was Christmas, and Kylie couldn't wait to see her presents under the tree. To an often neglected eleven year old, it was the one holiday she could look forward to, the one time a year when her parents almost got along. Why just last night they'd snuck off early and played music loudly in their room. She'd rather not dwell on what happened other than it wasn't yelling of the bad kind. To avoid being traumatized for life, she wore earphones to bed, the soothing ocean sounds lulling her to sleep.

She woke early and full of excitement. This year wouldn't be the letdown of the last one when her dad got laid off and they didn't even have enough money for a turkey. He'd gotten a better job soon after, and just last week, she'd overheard her daddy telling

Mommy that he'd left an envelope with cash to pay the bills with enough left over to get Kylie some gifts.

The hallway outside her bedroom remained quiet, the door to her parents' room partially ajar. Still sleeping? She didn't check. She hit the stairs and did her best to not race down. She wanted to savor the moment. She hit the last step and headed into the living room, only to halt, foot partially off the floor, frozen in disbelief.

The tree lay toppled, the angel that crowned it broken in pieces on the floor. Ornaments scattered all over. Most of them just broken shards.

Her mother sat sobbing and red-faced on the couch, bundled in her ratty pink robe, her mascara of the night before smeared around her eyes and running black streaks with her tears.

"Are you okay, Mommy?" Kylie treaded very carefully. Having seen her mom like this before, she knew her mood could swing a few ways. Most of them bad for Kylie.

"I'll be fine now that the bastard's gone." She honked her nose on the Christmas blanket lying over the couch.

"Daddy left?" That wasn't good. He acted as the calm parent, the one that shielded her if Mom got into one of her screaming fits.

"You going to whine about it? You shouldn't.

He's a shit husband. A shit father. And a shit provider. I told him I needed more money for presents. But he said he gave me enough. And now see what you get? Nothing."

The claim led Kylie's gaze to the downed tree, which didn't have a single wrapped present under it. A glance to the dining table showed it stacked with several cartons of cigarettes. Enough to last Mom a while.

She'd get to inhale secondhand smoke as her gift. Great.

Rather than explode, which wouldn't end well for her, she took off, ignoring her mother's yelled, "Don't you go whining to anyone about this, you hear me?"

Kylie heard. She saw. She wasn't stupid. Dad left because Mom selfishly blew their money on booze and smokes. Nothing new and yet it still stung. Not so much her mom's actions but the fact he'd left Kylie behind.

The chill in the air outdoors meant Kylie paused long enough to shove her feet into her winter boots and snare her jacket from a hook. Then she was out of the house, a house they'd bought for cheap when she was little because someone got killed in it. It was nicer than the trailer, but she still hated it with its gross brown and crunchy carpeting. Hated the bathroom with its pink and black tile. Hated her room with peeling wallpaper depicting trains. She hated trains. Hated her life.

Snow crunched underfoot as she traversed her backyard to exit through the gate that led into the park. She aimed for the swings that someone forgot to remove until spring. She threw herself onto a seat and swung her legs, the creaking of the chain loud and ominous. It matched her mood as she pumped, wanting to escape. Eyes shut, she pushed herself harder and harder, wanting to feel the lightness of almost flying.

She almost crashed as a voice startled her.

"Hi."

She lost her concentration, the chains twisted, and she dumbly let go. As she dropped, she suddenly found herself caught by a boy. A tall boy, who held Kylie for a second before setting her on her feet.

"You okay?" His expression creased in concern. Her luck that a cute boy would be the one to ask.

"Yeah. Thanks." She eyed the ground rather than him. What must he think of her outside alone on Christmas?

He stammered as he said, "You must think I'm like a weirdo for being in the park instead of with my family. I just couldn't do it anymore. They were folding the paper from the presents. Which were books. And not the fun kind but science and history books," he lamented.

"At least you got something. My mom bought cigarettes."

"You smoke?" he asked in a startled tone.

"No."

He grimaced as he grasped what had happened. "Sounds like we've both got epic parents."

"I can't wait until I'm old enough to escape."

"Let's make a pact to escape together."

That was the first time she and Gunner met. The Christmas miracle she needed. It became a regular occurrence after with them becoming fast friends initially, but as they got older, and hormones started to rage, they fell in love.

They formed a plan of escape. He'd enlist while she went to college, that way they could both concentrate while they worked toward their future.

A future where they'd be together.

It worked well at first. He saved money and bought her a ring. Popped the question. She said yes. They agreed to wait until she graduated and he'd finished his current tour.

Only he went missing. Frantic, she called for updates. Her messages went unanswered. When someone took pity and finally told her he'd either been captured or killed, she just about died.

When he was recovered, she'd felt such elation.

It didn't last.

He didn't contact her. No phone calls, no emails or texts. Just a single letter received on December twenty-fourth where he broke up with her.

Bah-freaking-humbug.

1

A HOLIDAY MIRACLE would be tooting handy around now. Kylie planted her hands on her hips as she glared at her kitchen ceiling. She'd just had the upstairs tub fixed, had done a passable job patching the drywall, and now the toilet was leaking.

It never ends.

To those who said congrats on owning your own house, she'd like to present the repair bills and the hours spent trying to maintain this cesspool by herself while also dealing with her precociously smart nine-year-old, Annabelle, aka Squishy.

Not thusly nicknamed because she had the most adorable cheeks as a baby—she totally did—but because of her obsession with the stuffed version sold in stores. Not that Kylie had bought many in her collection. Money was too tight for that. But

Annabelle's father—her official ex for more than six months now—wouldn't stop buying them.

He thought love could be bought. And maybe he was right. His daughter adored him, but Kylie wanted more than gifts when he was an ass. *"You didn't iron my pants." "Where's my dinner?" "What do you do all day?"*

The misogyny only increased the longer they were together. It was during one of his berating sessions—where she eyed her toes, her head bent in contrition to appease—that she noticed her daughter watching. Did she think this kind of behavior was normal?

What kind of example did Kylie set? Her husband, Howard, treated her like chattel, and it was during a lecture on how she should dress nicely for when he got home from work that she realized she had to leave.

I should have never married him.

In her defense, she'd still been heartsick. A year after Gunner dumped her, she knew she had to move on. During her summer break at home, she met Howard, a wealthy young man whose family owned the local winery. She worked at a restaurant at the time, and she'd been flattered by his courteous request for a date. One date led to another. Why not? He was courtly, a true gentleman who held out her chair, insisted on paying for their dates. Didn't push her for sex, even though they went out for months.

She liked him but didn't love him. Despite doing her best to not compare him to Gunner, in her heart, he came up short. And it made her mad. Hence why she decided to sleep with him.

It was okay. She'd not planned to repeat it, only she got pregnant. Totally meant to abort it, only he saw her in town heading into the Planned Parenthood clinic. Since she couldn't lie, she told him the truth. To her surprise, he asked her to reconsider the abortion. After all, it was early in the pregnancy. He then whirlwind courted her. He was charming and sweet, and the sex got better. She dropped out of college when she decided to keep the baby.

They married before she showed too much. His snooty parents never approved. She'd thought it wildly romantic that he went against their wishes. She used to think it was a compliment when he'd boast, *"You should count yourself lucky to have me."*

Not knowing any better, she believed it. She could slap her younger naïve self. They really needed to give some kind of lesson in school about how to recognize gaslighting and abusive traits. By the time their relationship progressed from gentle correction to harsh—and what he called, constructive

—criticism, she was too firmly entrenched to easily escape.

No skills. No job. No money. And a child she wouldn't abandon.

She might still be married to Howard if her mom hadn't given her the chance to get out.

A stage-four lung cancer diagnosis sent her mom to hospice, and while not the kindest woman in life, when Kylie visited, she told her what to do. "Anyone can see you're miserable. Leave the prick. Now. You need to start the process before I die."

"Wait, are you telling me to divorce Howard?" Kylie had exclaimed.

"Yes, and quickly. Then he can't get his hands on your inheritance."

Which turned out to be a mortgage-free house, a surprising seven grand in the bank, and a way to escape his hold since he wouldn't let her have a job. Heck, he wouldn't even let her get a cell phone.

Getting out wasn't easy. The moment she said, "I want a divorce," he threatened to take Annabelle from her. Thankfully his family didn't own the judge and custody got split fifty-fifty, which he was always trying to poach on.

"Mommy, are we going?" The light of her life uttered a plaintive query. Squishy had been looking forward to this day for three weeks now. The town's Santa Claus Parade. Nine years old and still pretending to believe. Kylie loved that about her child.

"Such an impatient Squishy. Yes, we're going. Get dressed in your warm stuff. It's cold outside. That means snow pants."

"But there's no snow," Annabelle grumbled as she kicked her way to the front door, lower lip pouting.

"Just because it's late doesn't mean it's warm. You'll thank me later." Northern Georgia could be nippy this time of year.

"Why don't *you* wear snow pants?" Squishy hollered as she sat on the floor to pull them on over her leggings.

"Because I've got more chunk than you." No longer the svelte teenager, she'd put on enough pounds to be considered curvy. Her ex hated it. Had constantly harped on her eating habits, advice that often came with choice names too. She, though, rather liked her shape just fine. She ate what she liked, and she could keep up with her kid and job at the restaurant.

"No fair," an exasperated Squishy sighed.

"How about some hot cocoa to make up for it?"

"With mushmallows." Squishy refused to call

them marshmallows from a young age, always insisting they were mushy, not marshy. It stuck.

"I will bury a mountain of them in there and give you a fat straw." Kylie might be broke, but she would never let her daughter miss out. Kylie remembered how the little things her mom did meant so much, especially since they were few and far between. Unlike her own childhood, she wanted her daughter to have a plethora of happy recollections.

"You are the best mother ever," Squishy declared as her abominable butt opened the door.

"Wait for me, missy. I'm almost done." Kylie poured the cocoa into an insulated mug. The mushmellows started melting the second they hit the hot, sugary brew.

She set it down for a moment while she pulled on her stuff. Warm gloves, a scarf, mitts, boots, and her long coat. The Santa Claus Parade was a slow-moving thing of good will and lots of cheer more than anything else.

Kylie loved it. Just like she'd loved it as a kid. It took having a child of her own for Kylie to regain the love of the holiday after Gunner and his letter on Christmas Eve so long ago ruined it.

She shut the door behind her and heard Squishy exclaiming. "Hurry, I hear the band."

They had only two blocks to walk, and a good

thing since Kylie couldn't afford to buy a car quite yet. Even if she did have wheels, it would have been tough. The road was packed on both sides, as people parked on every spare inch and walked over.

As she went to join Annabelle, she noticed her child had forgotten a scarf. "Give me a second," she hollered, heading back inside to grab it.

"Last one there is a rotten egg!" Squishy cried out as Kylie leaned inside for the scarf on the hook.

Only to drop it as she heard the squeal of tires.

2

It had been more than a decade, and yet her house looked just the same if a bit more faded, the blue siding more gray than white, the trim showing a bit of rot where the paint had peeled. The roof had been patched with no care to matching, but it appeared solid and not dipping or tilted.

The little bit of digging Gunner had done showed this was Kylie's house now, inherited from her mom who'd died after Kylie filed for divorce.

Divorce because she'd married another man. Even had a kid.

It hit him hard. *It was supposed to be me.* He should have been the man she'd spent the last decade with. The child she'd borne should have been his.

But he hadn't had a choice once he'd been captured

and changed from a regular man to a werewolf. He'd had to walk away. Or so he'd believed. Now... Now he wondered if he should have stayed and fought for her.

A young girl came flying out of the house, bundled head to toe, and yet not hampered by her layers. She sported a big smile and a joyful laugh. "Last one there is a rotten egg!" she cried out as she sprinted for the sidewalk. His heart tugged. She reminded him so much of another young girl.

The child headed for the sidewalk. Call it instinct, or just plain luck, but Gunner was moving, striding across the road, his eye on the cyclist riding his bike out of season, hamming it for a camera held on a stick. The kid hit a bump, and his bike jumped sideways off the sidewalk into the road just as a car crawled past. They both swerved. The cyclist veered into a parked vehicle while the car in motion rolled up on the curb where the child had been standing until Gunner swept her aside.

No one got hurt, but the little girl stared at him wide-eyed.

"Are you okay?" he asked.

"You saved me." Her lips parted to show off a gap-toothed smile. "I'm Annabelle. Who are you?"

Before he could reply, a woman came flying from the house. Kylie, who'd haunted his dreams, took one look and snapped, "You have a lot of nerve showing up at my house, Gunner Hendry."

He wanted to run away from the condemnation he deserved in her gaze. The key word being deserved. He'd done her so fucking wrong. He'd also never stopped loving her. Seeing her he realized he'd do anything for her to love him again.

"Hi," was his weak start to gaining that affection.

Her look lasered him. "What do you want?"

Not the right time to ask for a do-over.

"He saved me, Mommy." The little girl stared at him with adoring eyes. "I was almost a Squishy for real." She pointed to the car reversing from the curb.

"Hey-zeus, Matilda, and Johnson." Kylie's attempt at polite swearing had him blinking. What happened to the potty-mouthed girl he knew? "I told you to wait."

A lower lip pouted. "I'm sorry. I didn't want to miss Santa."

"The parade is today?" Gunner asked with surprise. It would explain all the cars.

"Yes, so if you don't mind." Kylie strode past him, snaring her child's hand in passing, a clear brush-off, but he'd been a coward long enough.

"I'd like to talk when you get a chance."

"About what?" Kylie snapped, letting her child

pull free from her hand to join others as they headed for main street.

"Us."

She snorted. "There is no us, and there's nothing to say. As you can plainly see, I moved on fine without you." She glanced pointedly at her daughter's wooly-hat-covered head. As if sensing their gaze, the kid paused and smiled over her shoulder at them. "Hurry up, slow poke."

He cleared his throat. "First off, I need to apologize. Some shit happened to me—"

"Watch your language."

He clamped his mouth before uttering a surprised, "What?"

"I try to avoid cussing around Annabelle."

"Uh, seriously?" He couldn't stop the incredulity.

The daughter in question turned around, rolled her eyes, and said, "Better listen. Last time I said a bad word, I lost screen time."

"Oh. I'll be careful, then." His awkward attempt at apology. The girl seemed satisfied and returned to skipping. He glanced at Kylie. "You've changed."

"Life does that to a person. Goodbye, Gunner."

Wait, was she seriously going to walk away?

She was.

He couldn't, so he stood at the back of the thin

crowd. Mostly people he no longer knew. A few he did and tried to avoid eye contact.

His gaze kept straying to Kylie and the little girl.

The tidbits he'd gleaned about the girl's father was his name was Howard Keeler. The last name sounded familiar, and further digging reminded him that when he'd lived here, the Keeler family ran a winery that specialized in ice wines. They'd expanded since he'd been gone.

A hearse went by emblazoned with a giant and intricate K with a big red bow on its hood and an upright coffin decorated as a tree on its roof.

Then it was a dry cleaner, Keeler's Jiffy Clothes. The racks were hung with holiday suits being groomed by paper mâché elves.

Then a tow truck, Keeler Wreckers, with lights that danced.

The crowd murmured in excitement when it came time for Santa, waving from his big red sled pulled by actual reindeer. On the side of the sleigh, emblazoned in fancy script: Keeler Winery.

But it was the man beside Santa that drew his eye.

Good-looking guy, blond hair trimmed short, wearing an expensive-looking suit and long wool coat. A fucking yuppy. That's who Kylie married. The polar opposite of Gunner.

Annabelle hopped up and down and clapped, squealing, "Daddy's helping Santa."

His gaze went back to the dude, aka the target. Despite knowing Kylie filed for divorce citing irreconcilable differences, he had to wonder. Did she love the guy? Was there a chance they'd get back together? They did, after all, have a child.

"Careful, Squishy," Kylie admonished, her hand on the girl's shoulder.

Keeler spotted her and grinned broadly as he leapt from the sleight. "Ho, ho, ho, where's my girl!" He held open his arms.

No way anyone could have the heart to stop the little girl from racing to her father. He boosted her into the sleigh, where she beamed. What child wouldn't, given a chance to ride with Santa?

Kylie didn't stop it, but Kylie also didn't like it. She pushed out of the crowd, stalking in the direction of the parade's end point.

Gunner matched his stride to hers. "You okay?"

"Fine. Go away," she spat through a clenched jaw.

"You don't look okay."

She whirled to glare at him. "And if I'm not? It's none of your business what I am. Leave me alone. You're good at doing that."

"I'm sorry for what I did."

She snorted. "Sorry was ten years ago. Now I don't give a cr—" She caught herself and said, "Cock-a-doodle-doo."

He couldn't help it. He laughed. "What the fuck was that?"

Her sour expression went with her stomping. He didn't have a hard time keeping up to her shorter stride.

"Your kid is cute." He tried for a different angle.

"I know. I made her."

"I never had any."

"As if I care," she huffed.

"Never got married either," he admitted.

"Imagine that. You dumped me and then remained a bachelor. Sounds like your dream come true."

He didn't know what to say. She kept twisting everything. "Your husband must be important to be riding with the big man." He wasn't about to admit he'd looked into her and knew she was currently single.

"Who says I'm married? Maybe I had a child out of wedlock because, you know, this isn't the dark ages."

"Uh."

"Why are making this so awkward? Like what do you think you'll accomplish?" she accused.

Probably too soon to admit he'd come to win her hand in marriage. "My therapists"—also known as his meddling army buddies—"seem to think I'm stuck in the past when it comes to relationships."

"Don't you dare lie and say you've been pining for me."

"I have."

"I said no lies," she huffed, giving him a dirty side-eye. "No way you've been celibate this entire time."

He felt his cheeks heat. "Not exactly. But it was never as good as with you."

She outright laughed. "Now you're laying it on thick."

"It's true. I never stopped loving you, Lily." His name for her because he'd always thought her a delicate bloom.

"Sounds like a you problem because I did move on. I married, had Annabelle, and made myself a life that doesn't include you."

They arrived at the parade's end and only a few seconds ahead of Santa. He saw Kylie's expression freeze when she saw her ex-husband's glance boring in her direction.

"You should leave," she softly advised.

"You're scared of him." It hit him with shock.

"He's looking for an excuse to take my daughter away. I have to tread carefully."

He knew that her custody agreement gave her a fifty-fifty share at the moment. "Want me to make him disappear?" he offered.

She blinked at him. "Tell me you're joking."

"That man is threatening you."

"That man is the father of my child. Now if you'll excuse me." She turned her back on him. But his chance to escape vanished as he heard the high pitch of a little girl saying, "... saved me from a car that tried to drive on the curb."

The claim led to a dark gaze settling on him then a fake, if charming smile from Keeler. He couldn't run now.

"Hello, Kylie. Who is this friend of yours to whom I owe thanks for saving our unattended daughter from being run over?"

"She wasn't unattended," Kylie muttered.

"Gunner Hendry." He held out his hand, and to his annoyance, the other man had a firm shake. Not a pushover.

"Isn't this the guy who practically left you at the altar?" A mocking tone followed by an insult. "I should have paid attention before taking the plunge in your stead."

"Not in front of Annabelle," Kylie murmured as the child's lips turned down.

Keeler set her down. "Go see my assistant and ask her if she has any leftover candy canes."

"'K." Annabelle ran off, and the man lost any veneer of kindness as he turned on his ex-wife. "If you are incapable of monitoring our child when in your care, perhaps I should have those privileges revoked. I know you failed at being a wife. Is it too much to ask you to be a diligent mother?"

Had there not been a crowd, Gunner would have made the guy swallow his teeth. He chose to use words instead of his fists. "Hey, man, that's a little harsh. What happened was a fluke, and luckily no one got hurt." Gunner interceded and drew Keeler's ire to him.

"You aren't involved in this. Nor will you get involved." Then to Kylie, "This man isn't to be allowed around our daughter. You know those ex-military types can't be trusted." Keeler's insult wasn't entirely wrong.

Lots of veterans came back with issues, but with a bit of help, they could surmount them.

Kylie ducked her head and nodded.

The submission had Gunner hissing, "Listen, asshole, maybe you've forgotten, but as Kylie's ex, you don't get to tell her shit anymore, and that includes who she sees or doesn't."

Keeler's brows lifted. "Is that what you think?"

"Gunner, you aren't helping. Just go away." She lifted her chin to Keeler. "I don't want to fight. I'd like Annabelle to have a nice Christmas."

"I'm glad to hear that because I'm taking her tonight."

"What? You can't do that. I'm supposed to have her until Friday."

"There's a city hall thing tonight that I'm expected to show for with activities for the children."

"She has school tomorrow," Kylie argued.

"It isn't supposed to finish late. Tomorrow, after her holiday school concert, I'm taking her to the company Christmas party. I'll have her back to you the morning after."

"You can't do that. It's not part of our agreement," she insisted, and it was all Gunner could do not to hit the guy in the face for upsetting her.

Keeler's smirk widened. "An agreement that can be changed. Never forget that."

With that, he turned and strode off, leaving Gunner to mutter, "What a prick."

"Takes one to know one," she replied before she stomped away.

3

I CAN'T BELIEVE he did this to me again.

Howard had forced Kylie into a corner where she had only one choice. His choice. He knew he just had to threaten to take Annabelle and she'd cave. It was a wonder he didn't try to use it to wiggle out of the divorce. Then again, rumor had it he'd started seeing a socialite his parents most likely approved of.

As Kylie stomped her way home from the parade after hugging and kissing Annabelle goodbye, she noticed Gunner took the hint and left.

The nerve of him showing up, looking as sexy as ever and thinking he could apologize!

Ha. That ship sailed a long time ago. She wasn't about to let him get close enough to hurt her again. She'd felt petty satisfaction at hearing he'd never married or had a family. Enjoyed the pained twinge he'd not hidden when she spoke of having done the opposite.

Did it hurt to know she'd moved on? Good. He deserved it after the way he'd crushed her.

She reached her sad-looking house, the only one on the street without Christmas lights strung. It's only concession to the holidays were the snowflake cutouts she'd made with Squishy taped inside the windows.

In her defense, she'd been working as much as she could, especially on the days Annabelle stayed with her dad. Not that it helped since the house kept gobbling her attempt at creating a slush fund.

Still, she really should do better for her daughter's first Christmas on their own. She'd have to brave the basement at one point and see what, if anything, remained decoration wise. They'd never celebrated after her dad left. At least not together. Gunner was the one to make sure she felt special not just on Christmas but all the holidays—even the most obscure ones like National Donut Day.

At the same time, she struggled with making an effort because she already knew Christmas would suck. Howard, of course, arranged it so he had Annabelle starting Christmas Eve right up until New Year.

Squishy, being an amazing kid, cupped Kylie's cheeks as she sought to not sob and murmured, "It's okay, Mommy. You told me it's not the day that counts but the people. We'll have our Christmas on December thirty-first. Me and you. It will be special."

That kid was special, and it hurt when she had to go away. Forget the fact they could call or video chat every day; the house seemed empty without her girl. Its faded and ugly walls taunted her with her failure.

Had she done the right thing?

At her dad's place, Annabelle had the perfect room. It was pale pink trimmed in cream with a canopy bed, white scalloped-edged furniture with gold-colored fixtures, a walk-in closet, and even her own bathroom. A place fit for a princess.

What could Kylie offer? Nothing close to as pretty. She'd transformed the upstairs sewing room into a bedroom, a cramped space that had layers of wallpaper she'd meant to strip, only she never seemed to have the time because of her job. Squishy said she didn't care, but she couldn't help but feel as if she'd failed her daughter.

Tears trickled down her cheeks. Holy pity party. She blamed Gunner for her being so emotional tonight.

Where's that bottle of red I've been hoarding? She

couldn't afford booze, but a client gifted her one for an event she helped cater. It was cheap, but free, the best kind of price.

The bottle of wine went with her out the back door. She skipped a glass. Fewer dishes and why bother when she'd drink alone?

She made her way to the tree at the back end of her yard, the spreading branches of the oak thick enough to hold the treehouse she used to hang out in as a teen. It had finally fallen down a few years ago, the rotted boards giving in to time.

Some of her happiest memories were within its rough plank walls. Walls built by Gunner. When their town had removed the swing sets from the park, claiming cost and injury, she and Gunner had needed a new place to hang out. They'd built one, using reclaimed skids, which he pried apart, saving the nails that they might reuse them. With his skills, and her company cheering him on, he created a solid little house. It became their oasis, plastered with posters. She liked singing groups and artists. He put up cars and trucks. They smuggled bedding and other knickknacks to give it a homey feel. The strand of solar lights he'd contributed provided the soft glow the night she lost her virginity to him.

The sex had been so good. Maybe he lied about

her being the best he'd had, but given her experience, it was true for her. Howard had been okay in the bedroom, but he never had the ability to make her toes curl or make her almost pass out when she came. She never got the flutters when he entered a room.

She took a swig of her wine, its bitter taste matching her mood.

Gunner was back. After all this time. Why? What did he mean when he said he was messed up? Just what happened to him while in the military? He claimed he'd been damaged. She saw no signs of him being injured, but at the same time, did he think her so shallow she'd reject him for a scar? Or did he mean mentally?

Didn't matter. She would have stood by him no matter—

"I can't believe it's gone."

Kylie shouldn't have been surprised to hear his voice, and yet she jumped, rising to her feet and shaking her wine bottle at him. "What are you doing here?"

"Same thing as you. Reliving the past. Remembering how happy we used to be."

"The past was a lie." A bitter reply.

"I'm sorry you think that because it was what I clung to when I was deployed. I wanted nothing more than to come back home to you. I dreamed of the life we'd have together."

"Liar." She took another long draw. "If that were true, you wouldn't have dumped my ass in a letter the minute you got out." He'd not even had the balls to do it to her face.

He was here now, though.

She took a quick swig of wine and then slapped him.

His head didn't budge. "Wanna try again? You barely touched me." He tilted to give her a better angle.

"No thanks."

"Hit me. I deserve it." He sounded sincere.

And it made her feel like a jerk, which only increased her annoyance. "There's no point. It won't change anything." Not to mention she wasn't a violent person by nature. Just look at how long she'd taken Howard's verbal abuse before fleeing. It made her wonder if she'd still be with him if her mother hadn't given her a way to escape.

She took another sip of wine that went straight to her head. It didn't taste so bitter anymore. She didn't offer him any.

He hung his head, hands shoved in his pockets. "It was cowardly to write that letter, but at the time, I didn't want you to see me. I thought I was doing you a favor."

"You mean you thought so little of me that you assumed I couldn't handle the fact you'd been injured."

"It wasn't like that. What happened to me wasn't something you could see."

"You wouldn't be the first returning soldier to suffer from PTSD." She wouldn't let him off the hook because he'd never even given them a chance.

"It's more than just that. There's a savage side of me I never wanted you to know."

"As if I hadn't seen it. Or did you think I didn't know you beat up Jeffrey Skinner for trying to grab my ass in tenth grade?"

"I was a little jealous."

"A little?" She giggled. She took another drink even as she wondered about going inside. She really shouldn't be talking to Gunner. "I'm mad at you." Mad he still made her panties wet.

"I know you're pissed at me, and I deserve it."

She hated the fact he kept saying all the right things. It didn't make it all better. "You hurt me." A plaintive admission.

"I know."

"Why am I so hard to love?" It came out a soft, choked whisper. She didn't cry, though. She'd done that too many times already, only to realize it didn't fix anything. She'd come to realize she was simply not worthy enough for anyone to love. Except for Annabelle. She loved her mother. But if Howard had his way, he'd put an end to it.

"Don't say that." A gruff exclamation. Gunner went to hug her, but she leaned away and almost fell over.

"Don't. Don't pretend like you care." She hiccupped. "You went away. And left me. I was all alone until Annabelle." At least he knew better than to point out she had her mother. She might as well have been alone.

"You must have loved your husband to marry him." His lips twisted.

She snorted. "He was very good at hiding who he really was. We only married because of the pregnancy. And before you ask, it was an accident, a good one, but not planned. It's the only reason we ended up together."

"In that case, I guess I can say he seems like a prick."

"He is, and I'm stuck with him for life. Yay me." She finished the bottle and swayed on her feet. "I should go to bed."

"I'll walk you to the house." He did more than that. He cupped her elbow, guiding her feet.

"I hate this town, you know," she confided in a slur. "Hate this house. It's like I'm trapped, and I can't escape."

"Give me the word, and I'll help you."

"I wish I could run away." But her custody arrangement was restrictive. She couldn't even leave the state with Annabelle, or she'd trigger a kidnapping charge.

As they went up the back porch stairs, she gave warning. "Watch your step." She lifted her foot past the broken tread. Just another thing on her list of things to fix. It would probably help if she had more than just a hammer and a multi-head screwdriver.

"Place needs a little TLC."

"You don't say," she drawled. "I don't have the time, know-how, or money. I just keep hoping it doesn't fall on our heads."

"You'll be fine. Place is solid. She's just a little run down." He gave the house more credit than she would have.

Gunner escorted her into the house, holding her steady as she kicked off her boots and dropped her coat. When it came to the stairs, she almost barfed on him when he swept her into his arms.

"Oh, you almost regretted that," she groaned as he carted her up the stairs to her room.

"Do you need to throw up?"

"No." She moaned the word, and the jerk brought her to the bathroom then held her hair as she proceeded to puke the cheap wine.

"Ugh." She fell back from the toilet and closed her eyes. A tap turned on, the running water lasting only a moment. He pressed a wet cloth to her hands.

"Wipe your face."

She scrubbed and tossed the facecloth aside, only to find him pressing a glass into her hands.

"Drink."

The water soothed her burning throat but did nothing to ease her churning head or insides.

"Let's get you to bed."

He knew to bring her to her old room, the one she'd had as a kid. She'd not changed it, mostly because her mom's room had yet to be cleaned out. She'd left it closed. One day she'd tackle it. Not today.

He placed her on her bed, the single frame just big enough to hold her. He pulled off her socks, but when his hands went to the waistband of her pants, she revived enough to say, "What are you doing?"

"Just making you comfortable."

"I can do it," she stubbornly insisted. "Go away."

"Let me help."

"No." Her obstinate reply as she turned on her

side. "Leave me alone." To her relief—and annoyance—he stepped away.

"Holler if you need me," he stated as he left.

As if she'd call for him.

Never again. Because last time, no matter how she screamed and cried, she remained alone.

4

Gunner couldn't help but sink to the floor in the hall outside of Kylie's room.

He'd fucked things up so goddamned bad. Hurt the one person he'd meant to protect. He'd not realized how much until he heard the pain in her accusation.

In his own misery about becoming Lycan, he'd not once thought of her own agony. He'd seen himself as sparing her. Acted like a fucking martyr when he was really just an asshole who'd abandoned the woman he loved.

In his defense, at eighteen, with no skills or prospects and not being a book-smart kind of kid, the military offered him the best choice. A career in exchange for a paycheck. He and Kylie had it all planned. He'd do a few tours and save some money while she got a degree from college. Then he'd ask for discharge, and they'd get married and move in together.

It was all going as scheduled. He was on his third tour. She was a year away from graduating. On his last visit, he'd brought a ring.

A ring she'd almost lost in her excitement to say yes. Kylie practically tackled him, and luckily, the ring bounced but didn't roll out of the treehouse.

He still remembered their last words.

"Promise me," she whispered with sweet kisses as they lay on the blanket spread in the tree house he'd built her so they could have a special place of their own.

"I promise, no matter what, I will come back to you."

He'd meant it. He would have done anything to return to her, but that fourth tour... Everything went to shit.

It started with his patrol getting ambushed. One minute they were driving the dusty road, and the next, the vehicle rolled, tossing Brock from his gunner seat and banging the rest of them around.

By the time Gunner found his senses and got to his feet, rebel forces—their faces hidden—had them surrounded. They were taken into custody.

The cell proved unpleasant. The food unpalatable. But it was the bite from a werewolf that changed everything.

When Gunner did finally escape, he wasn't the man he used to be. Oh no. He was now part monster. Part beast. A killer with blood on his paws.

When the military discharged him citing his mental issues—because apparently telling them they needed to get the wolf out of him sounded crazy—he tried to go home. He meant to tell Kylie everything.

Until he saw her.

The Thanksgiving break meant she was back home from college, or so he assumed as he stood on the sidewalk out front. He couldn't muster the nerve to knock on the door. Instead, he'd gone around back, slipping into the yard, unsure of what he planned to do.

As it turned out nothing because he noticed a flickering light. Keeping to the shadows, he avoided being seen by the sad young woman looking out a tree house window, a candle with a single flame flickering on the sill.

Waiting for me.

It slugged him in the gut. She pined for a man who no longer existed. Gunner had a wolf inside him. He couldn't give her the life she deserved. The child they'd both wanted.

The kindest thing he could do would be to set her free.

He never spoke to her. He left and took the coward's route, knowing she would never agree. And he wouldn't be able to resist if she cried. His yellow belly mailed her a letter to break up and gave her no way to contact him.

It was best that way.

Best for who? He didn't know.

But more than a decade later, he realized he'd made a mistake.

He sat in that hall until he knew for sure she slept. He could hear it in the cadence of her breathing. Then faced a dilemma.

She'd told him to leave.

She was also very drunk. What if she fell? Or had a medical emergency?

He headed down to the main floor of the small bungalow. A home she hated. He didn't see it like she did. He saw a place worn out, but with solid bones. Pictures on the wall were mostly of Annabelle. A baby with long lashes. A toddler with an engaging smile. A picture of her screaming and reaching while in Santa's lap, which made him smile. He remembered one of Kylie doing the same thing. It occurred to him that, despite being close to Christmas, she didn't have much in way of decoration. Make that nothing.

Odd. She used to love Christmas.

His phone pinged, and he noticed a call from Brock. He answered, "What now? Isn't it too soon for a reunion?" He'd just come from London where he'd helped put down a mad scientist.

"Can't a man call to say hello?"

"No. Because it's weird. You should text."

"I hate texting."

"And I hate talking on the phone so get to the point."

"We still haven't found her."

"Her" being Joella, the mad scientist's sister. She was married to a Cabal member, putting her in a prime position to cover up her insane brother's heinous experiments—aka genetic mutation done to people.

"No way she survived those injuries." He'd been there when the monsters attacked. Seen her go down. However, when the battle ended and the cleanup began, her body was nowhere to be found.

"Apparently, she's tougher than expected. And in added troubling news, sources have confirmed that a large sum of money was recently withdrawn from her account."

That had him freezing in place, finger

outstretched to the wooden trim that needed a slight sand and stain. "Are we sure it's her?" At least they knew her brother died. His ripped-apart body had been burned along with his monstrous creations.

"I can't be a hundred percent sure, no, but I thought you should know that whoever did pull the funds did so from a branch in New York City."

If it was Joella, that put her on the same continent as Gunner. "If she's smart, she'll stay far away."

"I think she's proven to lack the brains to do that. I just wanted to warn you."

"Thanks, brother. Have you heard from Quinn?" His other wolf brother had gone into hiding with Dr. Erryn Silver, a natural-born Lycan female who could partially shift and whose bite and blood did funky shit.

Given the Cabal decided she was dangerous, they'd put out a call to bring her and Quinn in, along with her father, Frederick, a Cabal member in disgrace, who also happened to be the guy who turned Gunner in that prison overseas. Talk about a small convoluted world.

"Quinn and Erryn are doing good. No idea where they've gone, but he dropped me a line a day ago to let me know they were somewhere safe."

"Glad to hear it."

"What about you? Did you talk to her?" Brock

turned personal.

Old Gunner would have told him to fuck off. Trying to not be an asshole, Gunner sighed. "Yes. It didn't go over well. She's pretty pissed."

"Did you apologize?"

"Yeah. I don't think she cared."

"How about doing something nice for her? You know that adage, actions speak louder than words."

A glance around showed all kinds of things he could do. Thoughtful gestures. While he toured the place, making a mental list, he made sure all the windows and doors were locked. Just in case, because as he'd learned, trouble had a way of finding him.

"She was pretty adamant about not wanting to talk to me."

"Good thing I know you're just as stubborn then."

Gunner snorted. "More like a masochist."

"Don't give up so soon," Brock advised. "Not all things come quickly." A reference to the fact he and his lady friend had danced around their own attraction for a decade.

"Never said I was calling it quits." Not this time.

He was going to do what he should have ten years ago.

Fight for the woman he loved.

5

Given Kylie fell asleep with Gunner on the brain, no surprise he featured in her dream, reminding her what it felt like to be happy and in love. Until he walked away from her, fading as he went.

She ran but couldn't catch him. She yelled. At least she tried to. Her mouth opened wide, screaming his name, only to have no sound emerge. He never heard her crying for him to come back. He left without a backwards glance.

Abandoned her and broke her heart.

Kylie woke to her alarm chiming and her head pounding. She knew better than to drink. Even one glass was enough to make her tipsy. A whole bottle?

No wonder she'd been puking.

Oh god. Gunner had been there last night. Apologizing. Being nice. Holding her hair while she puked in the toilet. The shame of it had her almost cursing.

She stripped out of her bra and shirt, pants and undies too. She stepped across the hall to the bathroom and showered quickly, feeling a tad more human by the end of it.

She then dressed for work before heading downstairs to the smell of brewing coffee. What the heck?

Inside her kitchen she found Gunner with a pot of fresh-brewed coffee and pancakes cooking on the griddle.

She blinked. For a moment she wondered if she'd had a nightmare about them breaking up. Maybe this was reality.

Then she saw her daughter's drawing on the fridge.

She sat down hard and used her hands to hold up her throbbing, hung-over head. "Why are you still here?" Apparently, he'd not gone far last night after putting her to bed. Like a gentleman.

Jerk.

"You were pretty wasted. I wanted to make sure you were okay."

"In some states, I'm pretty sure this is stalking."

"And see, I've been places where this is called friendship."

"We're not friends." A grumpy rebuttal.

"Not yet, but I'm working on it." He slid some pancakes in front of her, along with some syrup, a homemade version she'd learned from her mom where she boiled brown sugar and water until it thickened into a syrup. It did the trick.

"I don't have time to eat. I've got to get to work."

"You'll pass out if you don't. Take it from a guy who's woken up hungover more times than he can count."

"So you're a liar and a drunk."

"Told you I emerged a changed man. It took me a while to find myself again."

"I would have helped you try." To cover the admission, she took a big bite of pancake.

He dipped his head. "I wish I'd not been afraid."

She froze mid chew, the lump in her throat making it hard to swallow. She didn't know what to say.

He slid on his boots and lumberjacket. Finally leaving. She pretended not to care and shoveled more food into her mouth.

"Holler if you need anything," he said as he went out the door.

As if she would be fooled again. Last time he left, she'd screamed for hours, and he didn't come.

She rose from her seat and spat out the huge mouthful of pancake. It was too sweet for the pounding in her head. She went for an apple instead, which helped her choke down the acetaminophen.

As she brushed her teeth, a banging startled her, and she almost gagged as the bristles went down her throat. What the heck?

She spat and rinsed before heading downstairs and tracking down the source of the noise, which didn't help the throb in her head. It turned out to be Gunner in the backyard, wielding a brand-new-looking hammer that he was using to fix the broken step.

Smash. Wait, he was removing all the stairs, prying and chucking hunks of rotted wood, using the hammer when they gave him trouble. A glance past him showed a pile of new wood. He was fixing all the steps.

If she'd had any pride, she would have told him to stop. But stairs that wouldn't injure Annabelle when she went flying out the door into the yard? She wouldn't be the idiot who said no.

Besides, she had no time to argue. She had to get ready for work. She had a nine-to-three shift meant to accommodate her schedule when she had Annabelle. With Howard intending to keep her after school, she'd be able to work some extra hours. The cash would come in handy. She'd only bought a few things for her Squishy to go under the tree. None of them the kind to make her swoon. She didn't have the money for an expensive electronic toy.

Gunner continued to bang as she headed out the front door without saying goodbye. She owed him nothing. If he wanted to fix things to atone for his guilt, that was his problem.

Work kept her hopping enough her brain could turn off. The morning rush rolled into the lunch one. Only as it died down did Gunner enter and stride to a table in her section. Although she couldn't have said if he did it on purpose, as there was no way he could have known which section was hers.

She brought him a menu. "The soup meal deal is decent, but if you're hungry, go for Patty's Special Burger Combo."

"Sounds good."

She left to put in his order and returned with a coffee and a water. "Thanks for fixing the back stairs," she muttered. Her hangover had subsided enough for her to be gracious. Beggars couldn't be choosers, and she sure needed the help.

"I also replaced some of the deck boards, but it's only a temporary measure. The whole thing really should be torn down and rebuilt."

She grimaced. "Yeah, I'll get right on that right after I fix the toilet, the furnace, and replace the window that cracked."

"Your ex is loaded. Surely you got something from your divorce?"

"A great big wad of nothing. Which is what I wanted." Her agreeing to walk away from his wealth and even alimony was why he let her have partial custody.

"Sounds tough," Gunner commiserated.

"I've managed." She didn't need or want his pity. She left to grab his meal, and when she returned to check on him, he'd eaten it and paid, leaving a huge tip.

A bigger person might have tossed his pity money in his face. A person with presents to buy kept it.

She ended up working the dinner rush since she had no reason to go home. Her feet were killing her by the time she got ho—

An unexpected view had her stumbling.

What the fuck? Her usually dark house was lit up with Christmas lights, mostly. A section on the roof was dark, and someone on a ladder fiddled with the strand. Not just anyone. Gunner.

"Now what are you doing?" she huffed as she headed up her walkway.

"Found these in the basement when I was cleaning out your furnace burners."

"And thought to yourself, I'm going to be creepy and decorate."

"You're welcome," he stated, doing something that lit up the dark branch with red and white bulbs, clashing with the strand of multicolored that led into the flashing set. It was hideous.

"Annabelle is going to love it." If she got to see it. With Howard stealing her, Kylie would only get her for two days before she left again for Christmas.

"Does the dickwad often infringe on your custody days?" Gunner asked as he came down the ladder. Also new. Where was he getting the stuff?

"Yup. And before you say fight him, I'm lucky I have any days at all. As you mentioned, his family is wealthy."

"We could steal the kid and run somewhere he'd never find you."

"We?" She arched a brow. "There is no we, Gus." Her nickname for him slipped out. She used to tease him that Gunner didn't give many options since he didn't like Gunny. She told him he should have been named Gustave because then he'd be Gus. A dumb thing to say and yet it became their inside joke. And she was Lily because, according to him, she was sweet and delicate. As a teenager, she loved and hated it. She also used it as an excuse to chase him around, tackle and tickle him. Needless to say, that was how their first kiss happened.

"You're not even going to think about it? I'm pretty handy to have around." He offered a winsome smile that almost melted her resolve.

Be strong. "I don't need a handyman."

"I beg to differ. Wasn't just your toilet and furnace that needed some attention. I tweaked a few things and started a list of other things requiring some TLC."

"You had no right."

"Did it anyway. The electrical switch in your kitchen was especially a safety hazard."

"You got it to stop making that buzzing sound?" she asked with a lilt.

"Yes." He winced. "Any other switches making that noise?"

She shook her head.

"Well, guess I should get going now that you're home safe."

"Where are you staying?"

He shrugged. "I'll find a place."

"Where's your stuff?"

"I travel light."

It didn't take a lightbulb for her to figure it out. "You're homeless."

"Not really. I just haven't found a place yet."

Bad idea. Bad. Bad. Bad.

She held the front door open wide and said, "Welcome to Kylie's B&B. Free room and board in exchange for repairs."

His grin just about melted her panties. "Deal."

"And for your first task, I need your muscle."

He arched a brow. "My muscle is yours."

"Good. Because we're going to get a tree, and since I don't have a car, you'll have to carry it."

If she expected him to protest, she obviously didn't remember him because he grinned, the smile of the boy she used to know. "I will bring back the biggest tree."

"Not the biggest!" She squeaked. Her budget couldn't handle it.

"Can it be fat?" he cajoled.

"You have seen the size of my living room, right? The place where you'll be crashing unless you can handle sleeping in my mom's old room and bed. I haven't cleaned it since she died." Her nose wrinkled.

"I can give you hand clearing it out," he offered as they walked side by side.

"I really should stop stalling about it and get it done, but..."

"Afraid you'll get all nostalgic?"

She choked. "Do you not remember her at all?"

She used to complain about her mother often enough.

"Given your dislike of her, I would have thought you'd have carted all her shit off a while ago. What's the holdup?"

"It's me, cleaning up yet another of her messes. Of seeing the way she hoarded stuff for herself while I went without. Of getting to recall just how terrible she was to me. Which sounds awful. I mean the woman died and left me a house. If not for that, I'd either be stuck in a loveless marriage or in a shelter."

"She's dead. Who cares if you still hate her?"

"It's wrong. I mean she was my mom."

"She was a cunt."

"Gus! Language!" she huffed in shock.

"I'm sorry. She was a platypus-ing, donkey-riding, sour milking cow."

The insult was so ridiculous she couldn't help but burst out laughing.

"Am I wrong?" he asked when she calmed.

"No." She giggled. "You forgot to add in how much she always stank of cigarettes and gin."

"Don't remind me. I still remember her lecture when I came to get you for prom. She was so drunk I worried the fumes would get into my jacket and we'd not be allowed into the dance."

"I dried out my corsage and kept it pressed inside

a book. While I was away at school, she smoked it thinking it was dope."

"And you haven't set fire to her shit yet?"

She eyed him. "You know what, that doesn't sound like a half-bad idea." She hated how easily she fell into talking to him again, but he understood her. He'd been the one to console her when her mom puked all over the secondhand computer she'd scrimped for. He'd screamed with her on top of the water tower, both wishing they'd gotten a better deal when it came to family.

"That fire pit in your yard is overgrown, but it wouldn't take much to make it usable."

"Then think of it as one of your to-do things for rent," she offered.

The trees for sale were in the church parking lot, part of how they raised funds. As they wandered, him distracted by the biggest trees, she aimed for the scrawnier budget-friendly versions.

She came face to face with a woman wearing an eyepatch covered in rhinestones, of all things. Her black fur cap matched her coat, and bright red lipstick caked her mouth.

"Hello, dear," the woman said with a thick accent.

"Hi." She moved past her, only to have the

woman keep talking. "That's a fine-looking man you came with. Husband?"

"What? No, just friends."

"Rrreally?" The stranger rolled the r.

Discomfited by her odd interest, Kylie offered a fake smile. "If you'll excuse me, I need to make sure he doesn't try and convince me to get an oversized tree."

She hurried past the woman to find herself too late. Gunner handed over cash and shouldered a tree, not a super long one but definitely one of the nicer choices.

As she reached him, she hissed, "What are you doing?"

"Getting a tree." He hoisted it onto his shoulder and started to walk.

She kept pace. "It's too big."

"I measured it. It's a touch over six feet. Your ceilings are eight, meaning plenty of room for a topper."

Despite the shame, she blurted out, "You bought it from the expensive side. I can't afford it." She ducked her head to hide her hot cheeks.

He paused and looked at her. She could feel his stare as he said, "It's my treat. Consider it a thank-you."

"For what? Putting you on a couch? Making you work for it?" Tears pricked at her eyes.

"I've slept on worse. I need to keep busy, and the thank-you is for letting me back into your life."

"We're not getting together," she insisted.

His lips quirked as he said, "Not yet." Then he whistled as he walked to her house.

6

"I'm going to pay you back," she insisted as they walked to her place.

"It's not a big deal." While outwardly Gunner remained calm and even smiling, inwardly he seethed. Angry, not at Kylie, though. At himself.

She was embarrassed because she couldn't buy a fucking Christmas tree. A basic thing in his mind, and yet, he'd seen her browsing the shitty pine section when she deserved the most epic one in that lot. So, yes, he'd fucking bought it. After all, he had money in the bank he never touched. She wasn't the only one to have family die and leave an inheritance.

His mother died while he was overseas on his first tour. His dad, a busy college professor, dropped of a heart attack not even six months later. He'd like to say he mourned, but they'd never been close. He and his brother, the basement-dwelling poet, inherited. A bad thing for Joel, given he blew a bunch of it on dope and overdosed within the year. All that to say, Gunner had a chunk of cash sitting in the bank and nothing to do with it. Until now.

"You're already spending too much to help me. That wood for the stairs couldn't have been cheap."

"Neither is renting a hotel room."

"At least you'd have a bed and not a lumpy couch," she countered.

"I've slept on worse." As they entered the house, her holding the door while he carried the tree through, he changed the subject. "Who was that lady you were chatting with?" He'd only seen the back of her head.

"No idea. Never seen her before," Kylie replied as she removed her outer garments.

He trotted the tree into the living room, and she joined him.

She frowned. "It occurs to me I don't have anything to hold it upright. Would a bucket work?"

"I think we can do better than that. Pretty sure I saw a tree stand in the basement. Give me a sec." He trotted down the stairs and grabbed it, along with a dusty box of ornaments.

When he returned, to his surprise, Kylie wasn't in the living room. He set up the tree in the stand, gave it some water, and went looking. She stood inside her mom's room, fists clenched, one holding a garbage bag.

"Whatcha doing?" he asked, leaning against the doorframe.

"You deserve a real bed."

"You don't need to do this tonight," he murmured softly.

"Actually, I do. I need to stop letting her get inside my head. This is my house now. My life." She glanced at him. "And it needs a makeover."

"Well then, let me grab some boxes. Some of this stuff is probably good for charity."

By the time he returned with a few, she'd already started dumping the dresser, muttering under her breath. "No money for clothes for me and look at this. Tags still on this stuff." She tossed shirts. Pants. Silky pajama sets. Much of it new.

The closet was the same, and it led to her screeching, "That selfish cow! I was practically dressed in rags, and meanwhile, she was hoarding all this stuff." She flung a party dress with sequins at him, and he caught it, catching a peek at the price tag. Three hundred slashed to one fifty. And never worn.

"We don't have to give it away. Want me to get the fire pit ready?"

Kylie paused with her hands on her hips. "A part of me wants to torch it, but do you know what they could do with this stuff at the women's shelter? Even if it's out of date." She held up a blazer. "Someone out there needs this more than I need to be a pyro."

Still Kylie the good and generous. It killed him to see her so upset. At the same time, he was exactly where he wanted to be.

They bagged and boxed the new and gently used items. The rest got carted out to the yard. While he cleaned out the firepit, she made more trips, bringing down her mother's bedspread, still reeking of cigarettes. Her pillow. Hairbrush. Even the perfume she used to wear.

The fire burned bright and missed only marshmallows.

Every time she tossed something onto the inferno, Kylie would say a few words. "Always hated that shirt." With the brush, "You had ugly hair. I'm glad I didn't inherit it." The bottle of scent caused the flames to flare and reeked. A grimacing Kylie said, "Her perfume always made me think of a funeral home."

When Kylie ran out of things to burn, she sat in a rickety chair beside him, staring at the flames.

He prodded her gently. "Feel better?"

"No," she groused. "I hate her. And I don't.

When she was dying, I didn't get an apology for her being a shit mom. No sudden death-bed regrets. But at the same time, she knew I was in trouble with Howard. She was the one who pushed me into getting the separation filed and told me to move into the house. She said it was the only way to make sure I had something he couldn't touch when she died."

"She helped you escape."

She nodded. "And I don't get it. She didn't come to my wedding. She barely knew her granddaughter. If I hadn't brought Annabelle over a few times, she'd have never met her."

"Your mom had issues."

At that Kylie snorted. "Ya think?" She slumped. "When she was in the hospital, I asked her about my dad and the way he left."

The same day they'd met. "What did she say?"

"That he wasn't my dad." A soft whisper. "She lied to me my whole life. Turns out she was already pregnant with me by the time they met. She doesn't know who it was. Said someone roofied her at a party."

"Shit." He didn't know what else to say.

Her lips turned down. "Guess there isn't really a better word for it. It also explains a lot. Why the man I thought was my dad had no problem leaving. Why my mom always seemed to hate me. Why I'm so unlovable." She hunched in on herself.

He couldn't stand it. "There's nothing wrong with you, and while what happened to your mom sucked, she shouldn't have taken it out on you." He reached for her, meaning to offer comfort.

She abruptly stood and avoided his touch. "I'm going to bed."

He wanted to follow her inside and offer her comfort. Given her fragile emotional state she might even want more. She used to practically maul him after fights with her mom in the past. But they weren't a couple anymore, and taking advantage would be wrong.

"Holler if you need me," he said instead. He sat by the fire until it dwindled to embers then pulled out the hose to make sure it didn't reignite. Only then did he make his way inside, too restless to sleep.

He fluffed the tree but didn't decorate it, fairly certain Kylie wanted her daughter for that part. As he stood by it in the dark, he glanced out the front window.

A figure stood across the street. A bulky female shape with a hat that reminded him of the woman who'd spoken to Kylie at the tree lot. A woman with an eye patch that might be covering a wound.

As if sensing his gaze, the person waved and then

walked off, leaving him with a chill as he recalled what Brock told him.

No way had Joella followed him here. At the same time, he'd lived in the same village in Romania as her for years. It was very possible he'd mentioned his hometown. Would she really be stupid enough to stalk him? She had to know he wouldn't tolerate any threat to him or those he cared about.

He ran out the front door and across the street to where she'd stood. The scent left behind not one he recognized.

A part of him wanted to chase her down. She couldn't have gone far.

He glanced back at the house. Kylie was alone inside. What if this was a ploy to draw him away?

Rather than race off, he returned to lie on the couch, anxious. Did his utmost to convince himself he had nothing to worry about.

Apparently, he was a little more freaked than expected because he woke with an unmanly grunt when a little girl poked him and said, "Are you dead?"

7

Kylie had woken feeling oddly excited. Strange given she'd gone to bed feeling kind of down. Reliving her mother's revelation about her conception, how she was the product of rape, hurt. At the same time, it explained so much. No wonder her mother hated her. Never mind the fact Kylie couldn't imagine despising an innocent child. Rationally, she knew her mother's trauma didn't give her the right to abuse. But reality often disappointed.

She had to wonder if things would have been different if her mother had told her as a child. Why wait until she was dying to admit the truth? Then again, knowing this as a teen might have put Kylie on a different path, one more self-destructive.

It had been liberating telling someone her dark secret. To have him reaffirm the fact she didn't deserve it. So why hadn't she let Gunner console her last night? She'd certainly needed a hug, but instead, she'd fled. Fled as if she were about to do something stupid. Say, like allow him to comfort her. Being in his arms, close to him, she already knew what would happen. Might still happen if he kept sleeping on her couch.

She heard a car door slam and a murmur of voices. It almost sounded like Annabelle. She glanced at her clock. Almost eight. Her daughter should have been on her way to school. She bounced out of her bed, already dressed in a sweater and track pants, her hair a wild mess as she bolted down the stairs in time to hear Annabelle waking her couch-surfing guest with a precocious, "Are you dead?"

She walked into the living just as Gunner hit the floor, bounced to his feet, slicked back his hair, and stuttered, "Hey there, kiddo. Not dead, as you can see."

Annabelle giggled. "You sleep like a corpse." Then to show what she meant, Squishy closed her eyes and crossed her hands over her chest.

"Oh. Um. Sorry?" The poor guy sounded so confused.

"What are you doing here, Squishy?" Kylie asked, making her presence known. "Shouldn't you be getting to school?"

"She insisted on swinging by to grab something she needs for the Christmas concert." Howard entered, a disdainful look on his face as he judged and found lacking everything in her childhood home.

"Her jingle hat," Kylie exclaimed. "It's on her dresser."

"I'll be right back, Daddy." Annabelle ran off, leaving Howard to glare at Gunner.

"What is *he* doing here?"

The tone set Kylie on the defensive. "Gunner's doing some work on the house for me in exchange for a place to crash until he finds something more permanent."

"Work." One word and Howard made it sound dirty.

"Turns out he's handy, unlike some people I know." A dig right back, given Howard's idea of fixing anything involved calling and paying for someone to handle it.

"I thought I made myself clear. I don't want him around my daughter."

Kylie lifted her chin. "She's *our* daughter. And you don't get to decide who my friends are."

"Friends? You haven't seen him in a decade."

"And?" she sassed.

Gunner surprisingly didn't say anything, just remained steadfast by her side. She appreciated the fact he let her handle the situation while wondering why he didn't tell Howard where to go. While she didn't need to be rescued, sometimes she wanted it.

"I really have to wonder at the choices you've been making, Kylie. Perhaps you should seek some professional help."

"Me?" she squeaked. "I don't need a therapist because I refuse to do your bidding."

Howard's jaw tensed. "It's not wrong for me to ensure my daughter is safe when she visits."

"Annabelle is perfectly fine with me, and you know it," she huffed.

"I wonder if a judge will agree given your current living conditions." He glared at Gunner, who finally had something to say.

"Kylie's a good mom, and you know it."

"Mind your business," Howard replied tersely.

"Kylie is my business, and I won't have you coming into her own house and talking down to her like that."

"Or what?" Howard taunted.

"Keep pushing me, and you'll find out." Gunner issued a low threat.

Annabelle returned, waving her hat. "Got it. You coming to see me, Mommy?"

"I wouldn't miss it, Squishy." She'd taken the day off work for the school concert.

"Are you coming too?" she asked Gunner.

"If your mom says it's okay."

The look on Howard's face told her what she should reply. But she wasn't married to him anymore, so she popped a cheerful, "We'll both be there wearing the ugliest Christmas sweaters you ever did see."

"Yay! Come on, Daddy. We have to get to school. We're decorating cookies instead of doing math." Annabelle offered Kylie a quick hug and another to a surprised Gunner before flying out the door.

A disgruntled Howard's lips flattened. "We will discuss this further."

Kylie knew what that meant. He'd berate and lecture until she gave in. Only he had no right to dictate to her anymore. She found her spine and lifted her chin. "There's nothing to discuss. This is my house, Howard. You don't get to tell me who can come and go."

"We'll see about that." His ominous threat as he headed out the door.

"What a fucking prick," Gunner exclaimed.

While she agreed, her lips turned down. "I shouldn't have antagonized him." She sat down hard on the couch in the mess of blankets Gunner had thrown off at his abrupt awakening. She put her head in her hands as it occurred to her how that simple act of defiance might land her back in family court. Howard didn't like being contradicted.

"Just say the word, Lily, and he doesn't have to be a problem," he offered.

"What are you going to do, kill him?"

"If that's what it takes."

She glanced at him and saw his grim mien. "Wait, you're serious?"

"He's an asshole."

"He's also Annabelle's dad. You can't just murder him because he's rude to me." What had the military done to him that he even thought that was a solution?

"We both know he's more than rude," Gunner snapped. "The guy's purposely yanking your chain."

"And? That's my problem. Not yours."

"Yeah, well, I'm making him my problem because I can see he scares you."

"He scares me because he has the clout to take my daughter away. And having you here just gives him ammunition."

"Like you said, he can't tell you who to hang with."

"Don't be so sure. His family has deep pockets and friends in high places. If Howard decides he wants Annabelle kept away from me, I won't be able to stop him."

"It's not right," he exclaimed.

"No, it's not. However, it is what it is."

"Is this your way of saying I need to find another place to stay?"

The correct answer was yes. Howard made it clear he didn't like Gunner. At the same time, appeasing Howard never actually worked, and she really could use the help around the place. "No, but I need you to not intentionally antagonize Howard."

"Ah, man. But he's so fun to rile," he said with a boyish grin.

"You do have a knack. I've never seen him dislike someone so quickly before."

"You're welcome. So, what's this Christmas concert? And did you say something about an ugly sweater?"

"You don't have to go. School concerts are wonderful and torturous at the same time," she admitted. She loved seeing her own child perform, but the two hours full of everyone else's kids she could have done without.

"Are you kidding? Sounds like fun."

"You say that and yet you haven't seen what I'm going to make you wear." In the summer, she'd snared a few Christmas sweaters at a garage sale for fifty cents each.

A few hours later, after he'd fixed a few things

she didn't even know were broken and they had an early lunch of hot tomato soup and grilled cheese, which he declared delicious, she tossed a bundle of fabric his way.

He caught it and shook it out. His dropped jaw almost made her giggle. "This is epic." He held up the knitted sweater with the giant Rudolph face and pompom red nose. The garland in the antlers along the arms truly made it stand out.

"Please, we both know you're jealous of mine." She had a tree with actual ornaments and blinking lights sewn on to it.

He grinned. "I'll admit, it's kind of hot."

She snorted. "You must have really smacked your head hard in the military. Come on. We don't want to be late, or we'll be standing on the fringe. And just so you know, don't bother asking for anything sharp to jab in your ears. My purse is pointy-object free."

"Shall we?" He offered his arm for the walk over. The concert started at eleven thirty and was supposed to be done around one. Given it was the last day of school before the Christmas break, most kids would be leaving right after. She couldn't wait to get started on tree decorating with Annabelle.

Gunner's appearance by her side drew a few glances, especially since Howard made a point of glaring at them from the opposite side of the gymnasium. Gunner appeared to be enjoying himself despite the short chairs and the off-key singing and even appeared sympathetic to the kid having the on-stage meltdown as they got overwhelmed.

When Annabelle appeared with her class, wearing her jaunty hat and bellowing with them as they sang their songs, his leg bopped, and Kylie wasn't even sure he realized he'd grabbed her hand and laced his fingers with it.

After the concert, they didn't escape notice.

Chrissy Ferguson waylaid them with a sly smile. "Well, well, look who's back in town. I guess I see why you ditched your husband."

Despite knowing better, Kylie stiffened and retorted, "Gunner's only been back a few days and had nothing to do with it."

"Sure, he didn't. Do you remember me?" Chrissy, divorced from her second husband, fluttered her lashes, still looking as perky and perfect at over thirty as she did in high school.

"I do. Seems like you didn't change," he drawled.

Chrissy thought he flattered. "You know, we never did get to talk much since Kylie used to monopolize you. If you're looking to catch up, or have some fun, you should give me a shout."

"The only person I'm interested in having fun

with is Kylie. So if you'll excuse us, we have better things to do."

He guided her away from Chrissy, and Kylie murmured, "That wasn't very nice."

"Ask me if I care."

"Maybe you should have gone out with her."

"What? Why the hell would I do that?"

"Because it would have stopped the rumors of us getting back together."

"Well, we are technically living in the same house."

"As a business arrangement," she reminded.

"If you say so." He winked as he held open the door to head outside.

Howard was already there, waiting by his luxury sedan. Avoiding him would have been awesome, but she knew better than to run. She headed for him and pasted a fake smile as she tried to be a good co-parent. "Wasn't Annabelle great?"

"As if there was any doubt."

"Are you picking her up Christmas Eve morning or afternoon?"

"Actually, change of plans. I need her one more day."

"What?" She couldn't hide her shock. "I thought your company party was yesterday."

"That was the general Keeler party. Today is the winery one."

Her lips pinched. "That wasn't the deal."

"I forgot."

"How convenient," Gunner muttered.

"This is my week with her." She stood her ground.

"So you going to explain to her why she can't go?"

"Isn't it enough you get her Christmas Eve and Day?" She fought to hold the trembling, but her throat tightened.

"Tell you what, I've got a meeting with a big client on the twenty-sixth. How about I drop her off early and you keep her overnight."

When Gunner would have stepped in, she spoke up. "I'll agree but only if you also drop her off a day early on the thirtieth."

To her surprise, Howard agreed. "Deal."

"You swear?" She wanted a promise because, while he could be a jerk, Howard did tend to keep his word.

"I'm not the one who has a problem keeping his vows." A dig on the fact she'd initiated the divorce. Then because he just couldn't leave the conversation on a nice note, "Here I thought you'd be happy to have the time alone to spend with your lover."

"Gunner is my friend. Nothing more."

"Maybe to you, but he wants more, don't you?" The last part he aimed at Gunner.

"What happens between Kylie and me is up to her. And right now, that consists mostly of me trying to show her I'm sorry. I messed up. I take full responsibility for that. But I won't lie. I am hoping she finds it in her heart to forgive me."

"Forgive you so you can abandon her again?" Howard sneered. "Everyone knows how you left her high and dry. It's the reason why I went after her. Do you know how rare it is for a good-looking woman to have only been with one guy? She was practically a virgin. So tight. But don't worry. I've had years to work her in and taught her some tricks."

Kylie gasped, and her cheeks flushed in humiliation.

By her side, Gunner tensed, and she half expected him to punch Howard. Kind of even wanted him to, though she knew it would cause trouble.

Instead, Gunner chuckled. "Wow, your penis must be really small if you're so threatened by me that you have to insult the mother of your child."

Howard turned a shade of red that looked unhealthy. "Why you piece of—"

Seeing Annabelle skipping for them, Kylie

exclaimed brightly, "There's my Christmas Star. Squishy, you were absolutely amazing."

"The best on stage," Gunner agreed.

A beaming Annabelle had even Howard softening. For all his faults, he did love his child. But it wasn't enough to keep Kylie from enduring his verbal abuse. She could only hope he never turned his criticism toward Annabelle. She wouldn't tolerate him trying to stifle her spirited nature.

"I was so scared," Squishy admitted. "But then I saw you wearing that shirt." Annabelle pointed to Gunner's sweater visible through his unzipped coat. "And I knew if you could be brave enough to wear it, then I could sing."

"Hey, what's wrong with my sweater?" Gunner exclaimed with exaggeration. "I thought I looked amazing."

"You do." Annabelle giggled. "Promise you'll wear it tomorrow. I wanna get pics when we decorate the tree."

We.

Annabelle assumed Gunner would be there. A man she'd briefly met but already obviously liked. Of course, Howard didn't.

"If the lady insists." He sketched her a deep bow, which had Annabelle laughing again.

"You're so silly."

"More like addled in the head," Howard muttered.

"Ready to go, Daddy?" Annabelle asked sweetly, and Kylie had to wonder how much of the undercurrent she grasped seeing how well she'd handled the tense situation.

"Of course."

"Love you." Squishy hugged Kylie first, then Gunner. A child who'd already accepted him.

And then she was gone.

Gunner put an arm around Kylie's shoulders and leaned in close to whisper, "Fuck, I want to punch him in the face."

So did she. Instead, she said, "Want to go shopping?"

8

Not hitting Howard as he purposely baited Gunner took effort, but he wasn't an idiot or a hothead. For one, he knew the asshole wanted nothing more than for Gunner to let loose so he could have him charged with assault and have the ammunition needed to get him out of Kylie's house and life.

Like fuck would he give that prick the satisfaction.

However, he also couldn't not act, so Gunner insulted the prick right back and braced for a punch in case Mr. Asshole-in-a-suit did retaliate. Alas, the coward only knew how to fight with words. Which was fine. Gunner could handle it. But he didn't like what it did to Kylie.

Her red-cheeked embarrassment hurt him. Her

honor had been besmirched. He had to do something to make things better. There was a full moon on Christmas Day. He wondered what Keeler would do if faced with a real predator? Given Kylie's vehemence about killing, he wouldn't maul the fucker, but scaring the piss out of him... Sounded like just the thing to get him in the holiday spirit.

Unfortunately, it did nothing to help Kylie. She tucked her head and trudged, quiet for the walk back to her place.

As they got within sight of the house, she finally murmured, "We should change out of the sweaters so they're still clean for Annabelle when she gets back from her dad's."

"Sounds good. Hey, if we're shopping, we should grab some lights for the tree. I didn't find any that worked in that box I brought up."

They entered her place, and she headed upstairs to swap clothes. She glanced at him over her shoulder. "You might want to dress in layers," she suggested. "The bus doesn't always run on time."

He blinked at her. "Wait, you want us to take a bus to go shopping?"

"I need to get some more stocking stuffers for Annabelle, and I've tapped out the local shops. It's not a long trip. Usually only about half an hour."

"Can't we take a taxi?"

Her brows lifted. "That's pretty expensive. You don't have to come. I can go by myself." Stiff pride laced her words.

Still, a bus? Yeah, that wasn't going to work for him. Gunner couldn't stand mass transit. Too many smells and annoying fuckwads.

He had a better idea. "Is Rico's Garage still in business?" Rico used to always have a few junkers, vehicles people ditched because they cost too much to fix. Rico liked tweaking them in his spare time and reselling them.

"He does, although it's now Rico and Daughter. Why?" she asked.

"Because it's time I bought some wheels."

"Now?"

"Yes, now. I can't sit on a bus."

"I already said you don't have to come if it makes you uncomfortable," Kylie offered.

"You aren't the only one who needs to go shopping for some stuff. And fuck lugging it back."

"Language," she murmured.

He winked. "You are so cute when you're acting prim and proper."

"It's not an act," she grumbled.

"Really? Because I remember what you used to say to me in the tree house."

Judging by her pink cheeks, so did she. "I haven't

listened to Nine Inch Nails in years."

And when she did, she used to gasp out the lyrics while they were intimate. A young man, he'd fucked her to that tempo and felt like he could conquer the world so long as she loved him.

"I stopped listening to them because they made me think of you," he admitted.

Her head ducked. "I wish you wouldn't say that."

"Why not? It's the truth. And you know what else is true? I hate riding like a packed sardine with strangers. So let's go buy some wheels." He grabbed her by the hand.

"I—" She'd readied herself to refuse, he could see it, when she suddenly pursed her lips. "You know what, if you want a car, then it's none of my business, but I don't see how you can make it happen today. What about insurance?"

"I've got a buddy who can help me out. As a matter of fact, I'll text him now so he can get started on it." He fired off a text to Brock, explaining he'd be buying a vehicle and could he hook up a brother. He didn't bother waiting for a reply. He knew his friend would come through for him.

The garage was a brisk ten-minute walk from Kylie's house. Rico and his daughter, Tansy, didn't have much to choose from, a two-door Honda Civic with a rebuilt motor—because the previous owner blew it up street racing—a minivan that screamed family and smelled of Froot Loops, and an old Ford F150 truck in need of body work.

He expected Kylie to gravitate to the van, seeing as how she was like super mom, but to his surprise, she pointed to the truck. "If you're going to be buying wood and stuff, that will be the most useful."

She had a point. He'd had to Uber the load he'd bought early the previous day, and the driver only agreed once he slipped him a hefty tip. "You sure?"

"It's not for me," she pertly pointed out.

He consoled himself with the fact it was only temporary as well. He needed wheels today, and a dealership with something new would require paperwork and time he didn't want to waste.

An electronic bank transfer, a signature, along with a temporary plate took the better part of an hour. Time enough for Brock to pull some strings and have him insured, but only if Gunner did one thing.

"Smile," Gunner said, holding out his phone.

Kylie frowned. "Why?"

"Because my asshole of a friend wants me to prove that you're not imaginary."

"Why would I be imaginary?"

"Because apparently I'm an ornery dick."

She blinked. "No, you're not."

He shrugged. "Only because I like you."

As she blushed and her face softened, he clicked the pic. A picture he'd save because that was the Kylie he remembered.

It was late afternoon by the time they got on the road, the radio jamming Christmas tunes, Kylie singing along while he pretended to grumble.

They hit a good-sized outlet mall and shopped. While she might have been leery about him buying a vehicle at first, she did a good job loading it up not only with some last-minute gifts for Annabelle but with bags of groceries. As she explained, "I usually only buy what I can carry."

As if he'd let her carry a fucking thing. He loaded the truck, and he'd unload it at the house. Once they got there. First, he insisted on dinner.

"I'm hungry. What do you want to eat?" He gestured to the restaurants in the vicinity.

"I can make us something once we get home," she offered.

"It's almost eight o'clock. By the time we get home and cook it will be bedtime."

"You grab something. I'll be fine." He heard the lie and could already guess it was because she didn't want to waste money on premade food. He knew it because she used to do the same thing as a teenager. Since her mom couldn't be counted on to buy groceries, clothes, or even school supplies, Kylie's after-school job had to pay for it while saving for college.

She often refused to order food when they went out, claiming she wasn't hungry. Because of her pride, he never pushed. He was more subtle than that. He did now what he used to do then and ordered too much food. In this case, a foot-long sandwich and a massive fry along with an oversized cola.

He brought the food back to the truck and could practically see her salivating. He placed it on the console between them with a casual, "I wasn't expecting the portions to be so huge. Have some."

"It's your supper."

"I won't be able to eat it all. Don't tell me you'd rather it went to waste."

She stared at him before accusing, "You did it on purpose."

He didn't lie. "I did."

"You must think I'm so pathetic. I can't even buy myself a combo from a fast-food place."

"Because you're smart and spent your hard-earned dollars on groceries and presents for your kid. So terrible." He offered her a fry.

She nibbled it. "I have a bit of money in the bank, but I don't want to touch it in case of an emergency."

"Smart. And before you worry, this meal won't break the bank."

"You say that, but I have to wonder. I mean you've bought tools and supplies for the house and this truck."

"And I still have plenty left. I got a sizeable inheritance after my family died and haven't had much to spend it on."

"Where have you been since you left the military?" A casual question, but he took it as a good sign. She finally showed curiosity about his past.

"All over the place, trying to get my head on straight."

"What happened to you?" she asked. "Your letters and visits, you never mentioned having problems."

"I didn't have any until my last tour when I got captured. It wasn't a good time." His lips turned down. "I was all kinds of messed up when I finally made it back to civilization. Even my army buddies who'd been through the same thing didn't want to be around me."

"Didn't the military offer you counseling?"

He snorted. "Yeah, but I was too angry to talk to a shrink. Was convinced no one could help me."

"They hurt you." Stated not asked.

"Yeah. But not where you can see. Most of it was

up here." He tapped his temple. "I came back a changed man." More accurately, he came back a wolf. But he couldn't exactly tell her that.

"And now?" she queried. "What made you decide to return after all this time?"

"It took me this long to realize I was punishing myself for something I couldn't change. That avoiding my past was hurting me more than I realized. But I think the biggest thing I came to grips with was I am allowed to be happy. To have a life. That I'm still worthy of having someone care for me."

"Oh, Gus, how could you ever think otherwise?" She reached for him. Her hand over his, a small gesture. Yet it meant everything.

"I know I messed up. And nothing I say or do can ever make up for it, but I want to try."

Her hand didn't move, but she did duck her head. "I don't know if I want to, though. You broke my heart."

He could claim he'd never meant to, and he'd thought he was doing the right thing for her, but that would be him making excuses. She had every right to feel as she did. "I know what I did was wrong. I hope one day you can forgive me."

She withdrew her hand and tucked it in her lap. "We should get home."

They drove without the singing this time. However, it wasn't exactly an uncomfortable silence, more a pensive one. Something between them had shifted with their talk. For the better? He couldn't yet tell, but at least she was listening to him. And while he couldn't reveal the true reason for his being a basket case, he'd come as close as he dared.

As they pulled into her driveway, the lights he'd installed glowed, the timer having gone off at dusk. To his surprise, Kylie murmured a soft, "Thanks for putting up the lights. Howard said it was a waste of time and electricity. I'd forgotten how much I loved seeing them."

Never mind the fact her neighbors all around had them. He'd brought her joy.

"Next year, they'll be even better." It slipped out, an assumption he'd be around.

He waited for her to retort. Instead, she offered him a sweet smile. "I can't wait."

Out she hopped from the truck, and it took him a second to realize she'd not shot him down.

Fucking hell, this was going to be a great Christmas. He loaded up on shopping bags as Kylie unlocked the door to the house. She froze in the entrance, and he was about to ask her if everything was okay when she said, "Someone broke in."

9

Kylie saw the damage the moment she walked in, the hallway wall graffitied in bold red strokes.

Whore.

While she stood in shock, Gunner cursed. "That fucking bastard. I'm going to kill him."

"We don't know it was Howard," she murmured softly even as there could only be one culprit. It just seemed so out of character.

Before she had a chance to process and get mad, her phone rang with the devil's number.

She answered hotly, "What do you want? Calling to see if I got your message?"

"Mommy?" Annabelle's hesitant query had her closing her eyes and leaning against the wall unmarred by the garish red paint.

"Sorry, Squishy. I thought you were someone else."

"Are you okay?" asked her daughter.

"Yup. Fine. Perfect. How are you?" She feigned interest even as her gaze kept straying to the message.

"I'm good, but tired. Daddy just brought me home from the party."

"Oh, how was it?"

"Good. I danced. And ate. They had a cotton candy machine! So good," Annabelle enthused. "Daddy took a bunch of pictures and said he'd send them to you."

"So Daddy was with you all night?" she asked casually.

"Well duh, where else would he be?" Annabelle giggled.

Kylie's lips pinched. He must have paid someone to leave his rude message and ensure he had an alibi.

"I can't wait to see you in the morning," she said a touch too brightly as Gunner brought in the rest of their purchases.

"Me too. Grandma gave me some ornaments for the tree."

"That was nice of her." At least Howard's parents, despite not approving of Kylie, did love their granddaughter.

"Is Gunner going to be there?"

"As far as I know. Is that still okay?"

"Yes. I decorated a cookie for him in class."

"I'm sure he'll love it."

A male voice in the background was indistinct but had Annabelle huffing, "Daddy says it's bedtime. Love you, Mommy. See you tomorrow."

"Can't wait to squish you," she replied by rote.

As she hung up, Gunner paused in front of her. "You okay?"

"No." She shoved away from the wall. "This is low even by his standards." She stood in front of the wall with its ugly wallpaper and even uglier message. "I can't let Annabelle see this."

"Put the groceries away. I'll handle it."

She wanted to argue, but she didn't have the energy. As she stowed away the food, she heard him going in and out a few times. By the time she finished and returned to the hall, he'd already started stripping the wallpaper, first spraying it and then using a scraper to peel it.

She didn't see a second tool to help, nor was there really room for two of them to work the wall, so she went upstairs. The bucket of cleaning supplies in the hall closet had everything she needed. She went into her mother's old bedroom and started by spraying the mattress with a deodorizer. She then proceeded to wipe down the headboard, nightstand, and dresser.

The walls weren't worth touching with their layers of nicotine, which still reeked slightly. She sprayed them as well to neutralize some of the smell. A vacuum of the parquet floor, followed by a mop, did much to improve the situation. The sheets in the hall cupboard had all been washed, even the ones that fit her mother's old bed because she'd wanted to remove the smell of smoke as much as possible when she'd moved in. She'd just about gagged when she ripped up the horrid brown carpet on the main floor, revealing battered, but surprisingly intact wooden floors.

She made the bed, topping it with an old quilt that smelled of the outdoors given she'd dried it on the clothesline in the yard. Once done, she stepped back to eye the space. It really was a good size compared to her bedroom and had a huge closet now that she'd emptied it.

The furniture was old, but pure wood. While the dark mahogany didn't appeal, she wondered how it would look if she stained it a lighter color. Peel the walls of the faded rose-bloom wallpaper, give it a few coats of paint, and it wouldn't be all that bad. Then she could redo her old bedroom for Annabelle, let her choose the colors and everything. Give them both a fresh start.

She blamed Gunner for seeing her old home in a new light. Speaking of whom, she rejoined him in the hall to see he'd stripped not just the wall with the message, but the opposite side too. The pictures that had hung on it were neatly stacked on the kitchen table.

"Wow, you were busy," she exclaimed.

"Getting rid of that wallpaper was on my list of things to do. Figured it would look odd if I only did the one side. And don't worry, it won't look like shit for long. I'll bring you paint swatches tomorrow so you can tell me what color you want."

"Thank you." She didn't pull a false "you didn't have to do it" spiel.

"Are you okay?"

"Surprisingly enough, yes." The message had bothered her at first, but it was just words and not even true ones. She'd been with exactly two men in her entire life. Even if she slept with Gunner the day he showed up, she still wouldn't be a slut.

"Come, I've got something for you." She inclined her head and returned to the second floor, wondering if he watched her butt as she went up the stairs. He used to back in the day.

A quick glance over her shoulder confirmed that hadn't changed.

She flipped forward quickly with a pleased smile. Was it foolish to enjoy his admiration? Probably, however, that didn't stop her from enjoying it.

She led him to the bedroom she'd set up for him. "No more sleeping on the couch for you." She swept a hand. "Clean sheets. Although I can't guarantee the comfort of the mattress."

"I can't take this room."

"Why not? Is it the smell? I tried wiping down the furniture to minimize it and spraying."

"What? No. The room is great. Better than great, which is why you should be sleeping in here. It is, after all, the master bedroom."

"But I did this for you."

"Which is exactly why you should enjoy it," he insisted.

She stared at him being overly polite. He was everything she remembered him to be. Kind. Generous. Always putting her first.

"You make it so hard to remember why I'm mad at you," she complained.

"Sorry?" he offered, the corner of his mouth lifting.

"You should be." She stalked closer and poked

him in the chest. "I don't want to fall in love with you again, Gunner Hendry."

"I never fell out of love with you, Lily."

Looking into his eyes, she saw he spoke the truth and hated the fact that if she were honest, she was still mostly angry because she'd never stopped loving him either.

Never stopped craving his touch.

For a decade she'd tried to forget how he made her feel. Tried to pretend being with him wasn't all that special.

With him standing in front of her, older, his body filled out but still lean and strong, she couldn't deny her attraction to him.

Desire coiled low in her belly. A heat she'd not felt since the last time they were together. Maybe she'd built it up in her mind. Maybe it wasn't as good as she remembered.

Only one way to find out.

He caught her as she threw herself at him. His lips met hers without any clumsy fumbling. Passion ignited between them, familiar and not, exciting and terrifying. She wasn't the young, nubile girl he once knew. She had stretch marks from pregnancy. A few more pounds.

He didn't seem to care as his hands cupped her ass and lifted her to press against him.

Her lips parted for the touch of his tongue, a caress that ignited all her senses. She sucked on his bottom lip, and his fingers dug into her as he kept her close. Their tongues tangled, hot and enticing, fueling the heat building within.

The feel of his frame against hers had her grinding, her hands exploring the planes of his body, which was all hard muscle. She wanted to touch it. She tugged at his shirt, and he helped her to peel it, revealing his chest, the abs ridges she dragged her nails over. His pecs defined.

Her top went flying next, and as she grabbed the clasp at her bra, he murmured, "Are you sure?"

"Is this a bad idea?" she asked, pausing. "Probably. But I don't care." She really didn't. For just one night she wanted to feel beautiful, loved.

Would she regret it in the morning?

Maybe.

Would she want a repeat? That would depend on how the night went.

The bra hit the floor, and as he stared at her bared breasts, she had a moment of worry. What would he think? She no longer had the perky boobs of youth but the full mature ones of a woman who'd fed a child and gained a few pounds.

"Damn, Lily. You are so fucking hot."

With that reverent declaration, her confidence

soared. Her hands went to the buckle of his jeans, and despite it being slight awkward, they each removed the other's pants.

Once naked, she placed her hands on his chest and pushed, walking him backwards to the bed, where she shoved. He sat down and dragged her onto his lap for another kiss. Her bare bottom wiggled, and he growled.

"Keep that up and this will be faster than our first time."

She giggled. He'd been so eager for her that he'd spilled before getting to the main event. "As I recall, you recovered pretty quick."

"Only because you are the sexiest woman alive."

"Oh really? Prove it." She slid from his lap to the bed, lying down and beckoning.

He didn't need an invitation to cover her body with his own. Her thighs spread, letting him nestle between them, the coarse hair on his legs a teasing friction on her flesh.

He leaned down to kiss her, trapping the rigid length of his shaft between their bodies. Teasing really, given she wanted it somewhere else.

"I want you," she whispered. Words she'd never said to anyone else. Only he had the power to turn her on to the point she wanted relief.

"I've been fantasizing about this moment for so long," he said, the words feathery light on her lips.

"Then what are you waiting for?" She wiggled under him.

He groaned. "I am not rushing. I want to enjoy this moment."

"So do I." She raked her nails down his back before digging them into his taut butt. His hips jerked, and he panted.

"Not yet." He pushed himself upright with an arm, leaving his other free to roam. His fingers traced a path from her soft belly to the rounded swell of her breast. He cupped it then squeezed, drawing a moan from her. His calloused fingers tweaked her nipple, rolling it, pinching it, and she panted at the tingles it shot down to her sex.

He dipped his head and captured her nipple in his mouth. He sucked, drawing it deep, swirling his tongue, teasing her until she arched and cried out. He kept sucking, raking the tip with the edge of his teeth. It felt incredible.

He paid the same attention to her other breast, playing with the nipple until it was taut then teasing with his mouth and teeth until she practically whimpered, her hips rolling and begging for something more.

She didn't have to say anything. He'd always

known what she wanted. Always knew what she needed.

His mouth slid from her breast down to her belly, pausing only a moment to nuzzle her mound. Unshaven because she'd not been expecting this.

And he didn't seem to care. He made no remark but continued to the vee of her thighs, his head nudging them apart.

He sighed. "Fuck me, I missed the taste of you." He placed soft kisses on the inside of her thighs.

She trembled.

He placed a kiss on the core of her, and she bucked so hard it was a wonder she didn't knock him out.

He chuckled, the vibration of it stimulating against her nether lips as he went in for another kiss and a lick. She sighed even as her fingers clutched the bedspread, her thighs open wide as he explored.

He took his time tasting her, spreading her lips for a lick. Stroking her and humming as he tased her. He flicked his tongue against her clit, and she trembled. He applied more pressure, tugging her sensitive button with his lips as his fingers teased the entrance to her sex.

She tried to not thrust with her hips even as she wanted to grind against his face. He kept on teasing her clit while his finger thrust into her. He pumped in and out, adding a second finger as he licked.

When she came, it was loud. She yelled her pleasure and gasped. It felt so good. So right.

And he kept licking. Kept teasing, rolling her orgasm into something tight and aching.

"Fuck me," she gasped, the words slipping out as her need grew taut.

"Anything for you." Even as he spoke, he adjusted himself and slid into her. His cock thick. Long. And perfectly curved at the tip.

She dragged him down for a kiss, not caring she tasted herself on his lips, wanting the intimacy as he thrust into her. Her pussy clenched around him, trying to hold him sheathed as he pulled out.

Then pushed back in.

Out.

In.

They found a rhythm that had their bodies rocking in harmony. Her fingers dug into the muscles of his back, urging him to go deeper.

Harder.

He obliged, slamming into her, hitting that sweet spot over and over until she could barely breathe for the pleasure. Her second orgasm hit, and she had no breath to scream.

He grunted. And came.

The hot spurt widened her eyes, but the shock wasn't enough to quell her pleasure.

A pleasure she thought she'd imagined to be better than it really was.

Turned out, she'd been lying to herself. It was more epic than she recalled.

He collapsed atop her, breathing hard.

"You okay?" she asked when he didn't speak.

"Fucking right I am," he murmured with a chuckle. "You?"

"This is probably a bad time to mention the fact I'm not on the pill."

He stiffened. Not in an erection kind of way. Then sighed. "You don't have to worry about getting pregnant. I'm sterile."

The announcement shocked. "What? How?"

"I told you I came back messed up. It was yet another reason why I thought you were better off without me. I knew how you wanted kids."

"Oh, Gus." She'd been so angry at him and never once thought to wonder what happened to him. She cupped his face and lifted it for a kiss.

A sweet and tender embrace that she turned lighthearted with, "Pity we're not young enough for a round two."

"Says who?"

He showed her a second time how much he

loved her body. It seemed only natural to remain spooned against him afterwards.

What might have been a tearful evening turning into one of pure joy.

Kylie fell asleep wrapped in his arms, smiling and content. This was turning out to be a great Christmas.

10

Gunner wanted nothing more than to spend the night in Kylie's arms, but first, he had to ensure she never came home to a filthy message again. It had taken all his self-control to not lose his shit when he saw the wall.

Calling Kylie a whore? She was the farthest thing from it. But he'd seen the shock and hurt in her eyes. Something she should never have to endure and all because of a prick who couldn't handle he'd fucked up his marriage.

The truck rumbled a little more loudly than he liked, and he could only hope Kylie didn't wake, or he'd have to make up a reason why he'd slipped out in the middle of the night. Maybe he could buy something as a treat to cover his absence. Was there any place with flowers or ice cream open this late?

He'd find out after he paid Howard Keeler a visit. While his parents lived in a massive ranch-style home by the vineyard, Howard lived a few miles away in a restored mansion with white pillars at the front, a wide veranda that wrapped around, and many windows, all of them dark.

A man like him most likely had security, hence why Gunner parked up the road and returned on foot, vaulting the wrought iron fence that was more decorative than preventative. The trees and bushes provided cover on his approach to the house.

As he neared, he paused to take stock of how he'd get inside. The main doors would be locked. The windows on the main level? Mostly likely had contact alarms, meaning opening or breaking them would trigger an alert. On the second floor, he noticed a rounded balcony with French doors, but of even more interest, the window to the left of it was open.

Before he climbed, he tested for motion sensing lights. He palmed a rock from the bed around the bush he hid behind and tossed it along the path he planned to take. Nothing triggered, but he remained cautious and army-crawled across the lawn to the patio. From here he could see the floodlight aimed to catch people, but not animals, on the ground. Or men inching flat. Once he reached the wall, he stood and hugged it, the stone exterior not providing much in the way of handholds. Good thing he'd learned to rock climb during his time in Europe. Using great care, he made his way to the balcony, where, for shits and giggles, he tried the French doors. He'd honestly expected them to be locked. They swung open, and yet he paused, waiting to see if it triggered any alarms.

Nope. Foolish given the direct access to the master suite. Had to be given its immense size, ostentatious bed, and carpet so thick the man snoring in bed never heard Gunner approaching.

He stood over Keeler, grimacing at the noise coming out of his face. For this alone, Kylie should have divorced him. Keeler slept alone, the other side of the bed undisturbed. Had Kylie's head once rested on the pillow there?

Annoyance flared his nostrils. If she'd slept with this man, it was because Gunner let her go. And now Keeler would do the same.

Or else.

Gunner pulled a switchblade from his pocket, extending it first before pressing it to Keeler's throat to waken him.

The man kept snoring, so Gunner pinched his nose and covered his mouth until the body reacted.

Gunner removed his hand.

Wide eyes met his, fear filling them at first, only to quickly narrow into anger. "What the fuck do you think you're doing?" Keeler snarled.

"I think it's time you and I had a chat."

"You piece of shit. If you think I' giving you any money..."

At the erroneous accusation, Gunner shook his head. "This isn't about blackmail, but what you did to Kylie.

"I should have known she put you up to this," the man exclaimed. "She'll pay for it, and so will you. See how she likes losing custody completely."

"Wow, you are one dumb fucking asshole." Gunner pressed the knife hard enough a bead of blood appeared on Keeler's flesh. "Kylie has no idea I'm here. As a matter of fact, I'm pretty sure she'd be pissed if she knew."

"Then maybe I should tell her," Keeler spat.

"Fuck me, but you're stupid. What did Kylie ever see in you?"

"A man who could give her what you couldn't."

The verbal blow hurt mostly because, in some respects, Keeler was right. Gunner couldn't give Kylie a life of leisure and wealth, or even a kid. But what he could offer? His love and protection.

"You really should be careful what you say to

me. I could kill you right here, right now, and spare Kylie the annoyance of dealing with you."

"You wouldn't dare."

"Buddy, I would do anything for Kylie."

"Even go to jail?" Keeler blustered.

"Do you need help defining the word anything? Luckily that won't happen. You seem to have conveniently forgotten what I used to be. Or did you think all I learned in the military was to spit-shine my boots?"

Keeler finally looked worried. "If you kill me, you'll be the first person they suspect."

"You're assuming someone would find the body. I know this town, Keeler. I know where to drop a corpse and never have it found. I am also really good at setting the stage. I can see the headlines now: Depressed Local Businessman Takes His Life."

"No one would believe that."

"Wouldn't they?" Gunner taunted. "It wouldn't be that hard to sell. A few unsent emails and texts to Kylie, professing your love and asking to get back together. Maybe a post on Reddit talking about how you don't know how to move on. Or are you more of a Twitter kind of guy?"

"Good luck with that. My phone is encrypted, asshole." Keeler remained belligerent.

"Again, you seem to think I'm a novice. I have

friends, Keeler. Friends that could have you arrested on fraud charges by morning if I chose to."

"Go ahead and try. I'll tell them you framed me."

Gunner grinned. "No need to frame when we both know you're dirty, Keeler. Did you really think I wasn't going to deep dive into the fucker who married and abused Kylie."

"I never hit her."

"Abuse isn't just physical. She's scared of you. What kind of fucker threatens to take a mother's child away? Especially from a good one."

"She left me!"

"Because you treated her like shit. You had a chance with the most perfect woman in the world, and you blew it. Which sucks for you but is great for me."

"She hates you." Keeler didn't sound so certain.

"Not anymore. And even if she did, we'd still be having this conversation because I won't have you harassing her."

"I haven't—"

"Yeah, you have. Between taking her kid when it's not your turn, insulting her to her face, and leaving that nasty message in her house."

"What are you talking about?"

"Don't pretend." Gunner whipped out his phone

and flashed a picture. "You going to tell me you didn't write this?"

Howard's mouth rounded. "You think I did that? I'm not a juvenile punk. And besides, when would I have done it? I was with Annabelle at the company party until we came home, and I haven't left."

"Bullshit."

"Ask anyone there. The longest I was gone would have been five minutes to take a piss."

"So you were smart enough to have an alibi while someone else did your dirty work. How much did it cost you?"

"Are you insane? I don't hire thugs to accost women."

Gunner wanted to call him a liar, but he could tell the fucker told the truth. "Maybe it was someone in your family."

"Are you accusing my parents?" Keeler had an incredulous note. "Because I'll tell you right now, they are overjoyed we split. My family never wanted us to get married. Their advice to me was to have Kylie abort and, if she refused, offer her money in exchange for Annabelle."

"Kylie would have never agreed."

"I know. Why do you think I married her?"

"Why did you marry her if you were just going to be a jerk?"

"It didn't start out that way," Keeler grumbled. "I tried, but I was never good enough for her because, even after what you did, she was pining for you."

"Kylie hated me."

"So she claimed, and yet I knew I never lived up to the memories she had of you."

"Because I am an original, and I am also here to stay, so we're going to need some ground rules. Starting with, insult Kylie again and you won't live to regret it. Two, no more taking the kid unless it's your turn. Three, no more fucking sending your goons or family or whoever it is to leave nasty messages. Do I make myself clear?"

"Very." A tight reply. "However, I swear on my daughter's life, I had nothing to do with what happened at Kylie's house."

"If not you, then who?"

"Maybe someone else isn't happy you came back."

The statement made his blood run cold. Could they have been wrong about who left the graffiti? He had to get back to Kylie ASAP.

"One last thing, you talk to the cops, or even get me thrown in jail, and you still won't be safe because my friends already know about you. And I'm a sweet ol' boy compared to them."

Not entirely true, but between Brock and

Quinn, he knew they'd spring him if he ended up behind bars.

"And to think Kylie chose you over me," was Keeler's reply.

"I didn't hear a 'yes, sir.'"

"Whatever. I'll have Annabelle back to her mother's in the morning. And I won't say a word, but mark mine, if you try and take my daughter, or harm her in any way, I won't give a shit about the consequences to me. I will take you out."

Gunner could almost respect the guy. Then he remembered he'd seen Kylie naked and worse? Touched her.

Before he changed his mind and slit Howard's throat, he left, moving more rapidly than his arrival because anxiety suddenly intruded. If Keeler had not left the message, who had?

His blood ran cold as it occurred to him. Could it be Joella? She would certainly have a bone to pick with him, and what better way to hurt Gunner than to go after Kylie?

He gunned the truck back to the house, arriving to find it looking just as dark as when he left. Upon entering, he didn't smell anything amiss, but he still took the stairs quickly, suddenly panicked that she might have been attacked while he was out.

To his relief, she remained in bed, and he slid in

beside her. She rolled in her sleep and nuzzled into him, even murmured his name as she complained, "Why's it so cold, Gus?"

"Sorry, I kicked off the blankets. Go back to sleep."

"M'kay," she murmured before slipping back into slumber.

But he wasn't so lucky, as he suddenly worried he might have brought trouble to her doorstep.

11

Waking up in Gunner's arms, Kylie waited for the regret.

It didn't hit.

What she did feel?

Aroused. Again. She wiggled, and lo and behold, she wasn't the only one who woke up interested. Gunner played with her until she was slick and panting before sliding into her from behind, his gentle rocking still managing to make her peak and cry out.

When the trembling was over, she sighed. "I need to get up and shower. Annabelle will be here soon."

"And I've got to get some painting supplies." He kissed her on the neck. "So get moving." He nipped her, and she giggled.

"I will, but I might need someone to wash my back," she boldly asked.

"If I shower with you, we'll both end up back in this bed."

She sighed. "Good point."

"Not saying that's a bad thing, but I know you're probably not ready for your kid to know about us yet."

Us?

She'd not even thought that far ahead. She'd been so immersed in rediscovering her sexuality that she'd forgotten about the fact she wasn't some teenager in love but a mom whose ex was going to show up with her kid, most likely within the next hour.

"Schnizzle sticks. I gotta get moving." She jumped out of bed and, rather than look for her scattered clothes, headed for the door to reach the bathroom.

"Damn that's one sexy ass." He whistled.

She cast him a coy glance over her shoulder. "I know. Sure you don't want to help me wash it?"

He groaned. "Killing me, Lily."

She laughed, feeling lighter and more carefree than she recalled in a long time. Despite his warning about them ending up back in bed, he did join her in the shower, giving her a tongue bath under the hot spray that left her weak-kneed and leaning against the cold tile.

They headed downstairs together and shared a quick breakfast of scrambled eggs with cheese and toast.

He headed for the hallway for a look, taking a pad and pen with him to write a list of things he wanted to grab.

"Any idea on color?" he asked as she joined him, cradling a mug of tea.

"You're going to laugh."

"Try me."

"White."

"White?" he offered skeptically.

"I know, you think it's boring and plain. And that's exactly what I want." She gestured. "My childhood was a mishmash of wallpaper and hideous colors that I doubt were ever in style. When I lived with Howard, everything was beige and gray with bright accent walls in each room. I just want simple. A clean slate if you please."

He nodded. "I think white will brighten up this hall and make it look bigger. Any preference on finish? Eggshell, semi satin, gloss."

"Semi satin please. I hate eggshell. You can't wash jellied handprints off it." She grimaced remembering Howard's displeasure when he'd come home to see the discoloration left behind. At least he'd only gotten mad at Kylie, not Annabelle.

"What about the bedroom upstairs? Should I grab a giant bucket of white for now and just start putting it all over?"

"Oh, that would be amazing." She beamed, and he leaned in for a kiss just as the door opened and a lively little girl burst in.

"Mommy, I'm— Oh." The surprised sound was followed by a giggle.

Then Howard's less-pleasant voice. "Get inside before you catch a chill."

Howard showed up behind Annabelle, dark circles under his eyes, his expression more rigid than usual. His gaze hit Gunner, and Kylie expected a rude comment. In a huge surprise, he held his tongue. His glance went to the stripped hallway, and she expected to see him smirk, only he remained placid faced as he said, "About time you redecorated. If you need extra furniture, we've still got the old dining set we stored in the basement."

She just about fell over in shock. Howard being nice? That would be a first since she'd gone through with the divorce.

"Um, thanks, but I think we'll be fine. Just going to deal with some cosmetic stuff for the moment."

"Okay. Let me know if you change your mind."

He then turned to Annabelle, who stood clutching her bag. "Love you, Squishy bear. I'll be back to grab you Christmas Eve."

"Call you later, Daddy." Annabelle gave him a big hug, and then Howard was gone without one single insult.

A Christmas miracle.

Annabelle dug into her bag for a sealed container. "Gunner, I brought you something." Out emerged a cookie with so many sprinkles it should have been illegal. "I decorated it myself," she announced proudly, handing it over.

He took it like a champ and ate it right there, exclaiming it was the best thing ever. At least he didn't fall into a sugar coma or grow a Pinocchio nose.

"Ready to decorate the tree?" Annabelle asked, all bright-eyed and excited.

"I actually was going to run to the store real quick to grab some painting stuff. But I'll be back within the hour, so be sure to save some ornaments for me."

"You can do the angel on top since you're tall."

Kylie's face fell. "I'm sorry, Squishy. I don't know if we've got a tree topper in the box."

"Don't worry. Grandma gave me one." Annabelle patted her bag.

"Then it would be my honor to help you crown the tree." He put a hand on his chest then winked. "So there's a donut store by the hardware store. I don't suppose you like them?"

"Yes!" was the enthusiastic reply. "Especially the sprinkle ones."

"Excellent. I shall be back soon. Need anything else while I'm out?" he asked Kylie.

He'd already given her more than she thought she'd ever have. "I think we're good."

He left, and Annabelle adopted a less-than-innocent tone as she said, "So, is Gunner your boyfriend?"

"Uh..." How to answer when Annabelle had seen the kiss? And what of tonight? Would Kylie pretend they weren't sleeping together and sneak in? Because no way did she want to be alone.

"It's okay if you are. Daddy has a girlfriend. Kind of. I don't think he likes Julia as much as Grandma does, though."

She just about choked. Her child was much too observant. "Gunner and I are still figuring out what we are." And then, because Annabelle deserved the truth, "We used to date when I was in school."

"I know. I remember seeing him in the photo album."

She blinked. "Wait, what album?"

"The one in the bookcase, silly." Annabelle rolled her eyes.

She then went to said bookcase and opened the cabinet on the bottom, pulling out an album Kylie had thought long gone. When Gunner dumped her via letter, she'd destroyed all kinds of things in her pain, but the album survived because she'd been unable to find it. Her mother claimed to have tossed it when she was cleaning. Which she should have known for a lie since her mom never cleaned.

It flipped open to a picture of Kylie and Gunner dressed for the prom. Annabelle pointed. "See. He looks almost the same." A boy grown into a man.

Kylie sank on the couch as Annabelle kept flipping, making her relive the past she'd done her best to forget. The concert tickets for *The Nutcracker*, a gift from Gunner despite him hating that kind of thing. But he'd bought her fifth-row seats and dressed up for the occasion.

Then there was the strip of images from the fair with them sticking out their tongues in the first few before sharing a kiss in the last one.

"You never told me you found it," she said softly. "You must have had so many questions."

Annabelle shrugged. "You were busy, and I didn't want to make you sadder."

She hugged her daughter tight. "Never be afraid to ask me anything."

"Do you love him?"

"I did."

"What about now?"

"It's complicated. But at the same time, how I feel about him doesn't matter, because you're the most important person to me."

"I like him. And so do you."

She did, but she was also afraid. Afraid to let herself love him in case he turned around and left her again.

That line of thinking threatened to burst her happy bubble. She changed the subject. "What do you say we get started on this tree?"

"Yes!" Annabelle clapped her hands.

By the time Gunner returned, there were Christmas tunes playing, ornaments hung at random, Annabelle had her Christmas hat with bells, and Kylie wore some ratty antlers on her head.

Gunner entered bearing a box that he set in the hall before whistling. "It's beginning to look like Christmas in here."

"I found you something." Annabelle proudly presented the elf hat with ears, and he popped it onto his head with a grin.

"How do I look?"

Her daughter put a hand over her mouth as she giggled.

"Hold on, I have more stuff." He went back out and returned, this time with a tray of hot drinks and a box of donuts.

"Oooh." Annabelle dove on the offerings, and with sticky fingers and much laughter, they finished decorating the tree. Gunner helped string the lights, his added height making sure they went right to the top. Rather than put the angel on himself, Gunner lifted Annabelle so she could place it.

Her impressionable daughter was wide-eyed with hero worship as she said in a not-so-quiet whisper, "He's really strong."

He was also a hard worker. While Kylie made them a light lunch, he applied quick-drying putty to the holes in the wall in the hall. After lunch, he did a light sand while she and Annabelle taped off the floor and fixtures, her kid treating the work as a grand project. Then it was time to paint. He'd bought the kind that didn't stink when applied, safe for use indoors and human sniffing. She didn't even want to think of how much it cost.

While Kylie prepped for dinner that night, a pasta casserole that would make great leftovers, Annabelle helped Gunner. She trimmed the parts she could reach while he applied the roller. They chatted away, and Kylie listened in as her daughter questioned him about pretty much everything.

Do you have a pet? Do you want a pet? Do you like dogs? What about cats? What's your favorite ice cream? Apparently, the pair of them unanimously agreed that anything other than chocolate was a waste.

When the first coat was done, Gunner headed up stairs to prep the bedroom so he could paint in the morning. She and Annabelle snuggled on the couch to watch *Arthur's Christmas*.

Midafternoon, she made popcorn for Annabelle to eat and string. She brought a bowl of it plus a drink up to Gunner.

She felt guilty as she walked into the bedroom to see he'd stripped all the wallpaper and was already applying putty to holes. "I should be helping you," she stated.

"You should be hanging with Annabelle. This is part of our deal, remember?" He indicated the bare walls.

"That was before. When I was mad at you."

He offered her a crooked grin. "Does that mean I'm out of the doghouse?"

"Maybe." She pretended to be coy.

He laughed. "If I were you, I'd hold out until I've retiled the bathroom."

She blinked at him. "You can do that?"

"Yup, because you're not the only one who isn't crazy about the pink ceramic. But I'll have to get a second shower installed in the basement first since it will take about a week to gut and redo the one on the second floor."

"My dad used to talk about wanting to put a second bathroom in." The word "dad" slipped out, and she cringed.

He grabbed her hands and squeezed. "Hey, no making that face. He was your dad."

"Not biologically."

"But he did raise you until you were eleven. It counts."

She sighed. "Does it? I mean he left without a word."

"Because he's a dick, but that's a whole other problem."

"Sometimes I worry about Annabelle. That by divorcing Howard, she'll end up feeling abandoned too."

Gunner rubbed his chin. "Much as I don't like the guy, he really does love that kid."

"For now, but what if he remarries? Or has another child?"

"Then she'll still have an amazing mom."

"You are just full of compliments." She stepped

close enough she had to tilt her head to hold his gaze. "Thanks for the donuts and the paint."

"Thank you for being awesome." He dropped a kiss on her lips.

"We're about to start watching *A Christmas Story* if you'd like to join us," she offered.

"Ha, I haven't seen that in ages. Hell yeah. Just give me a second to put my stuff out of the way." She gave him a hand closing the putty container and piling everything in a corner.

As they headed downstairs, they caught Annabelle closing the front door. Probably some kind of charity demanding money during the time of giving.

"Someone dropped off a present." Annabelle waved the small box in her hand.

Kylie frowned. "A present? From who?"

"Some lady with an eyepatch gave it to me. Said it was for Gunner."

"Me?" He sounded surprised.

As for Kylie, she couldn't help but remember the lady from the tree lot. The one with the eye patch who'd seemed so interested in her and Gunner.

"She even knew your name." Annabelle nodded. "I told her you were upstairs, and I'd go get you, but she said she was in a hurry and to give you this." She handed over the box, and Kylie wondered why he appeared so tense.

"Aren't you going to open it?" Annabelle practically shook in excitement.

He eyed it as if it were a grenade. Kylie reached over and snatched it, pulling off the lid to reveal an ornament. "Hunh. Wonder why the fancy box?" She held up an unpainted wooden cutout of a wolf on a string.

Gunner blanched. "I'll be back." He slammed his feet into his boots without lacing and bolted out the door.

Poor Annabelle bit her lower lip. "Did I do something wrong?"

"Of course not, sweetheart. I think Gunner's just hoping he can catch whoever it was to say thank you."

"He forgot his coat." Annabelle pointed to it on the rack.

"So he did. I'll bring it to him. Why don't you string some popcorn for the tree while you're waiting for us to watch the movie?"

"Okay."

Kylie put on her coat and boots before snaring his and exiting the house. A glance up the street showed Gunner standing on the corner, hands on his hips, looking left and right. She trudged for him, and when he whirled, she held out his jacket.

"Kind of chilly to be outside without it," she commented.

"Yeah. I was hoping to find the woman who came knocking."

"No luck?"

His lips pursed. "She must have hopped into a car, because I'm not finding a scent."

She arched a brow. "A scent? What are you, a bloodhound now? Is that how they taught you to track in the military?"

He gaped at her for a moment before clearing his throat. "Something like that."

"You going to explain what just happened? Why you freaked out when you saw the ornament?"

His lips flattened. "It's complicated."

"Complicated how?"

He rubbed a hand over his face. "I want to explain, but you'll think I'm crazy."

"As opposed to thinking you're a jerk for acting mysterious? Who was that woman? Why did you look like you wanted to puke?"

"First off, let me just say, I'm not sure it's her."

"Her who?" she snapped. "Girlfriend? Wife?"

"Nothing like that," he hastily replied. "Far from it."

"Then who is she?" she asked through gritted teeth. "And why is she coming to my house, leaving stuff and taking off? Exactly what kind of trouble are you in?"

"Recently, I was involved in a situation where Joella, the woman I think came to your house, was injured and her brother killed."

"Because of you?"

"Yes and no. She and her brother were doing bad things. Like really bad things. She was injured in the altercation to take them down and escaped."

Her mouth opened and shut for a minute. "Wait a second, are you saying she's a criminal who's hunted you down for revenge?"

He paused before nodding. "If it's her, then yes."

She blinked. "Is she dangerous?"

"I don't know. Maybe?" He shifted his weight from foot to foot and spread his hands. "The Joella I thought I knew was mostly harmless."

"Mostly doesn't mean not." She glanced back at her house. "I don't like this, Gunner."

"I swear, I had no idea she'd come looking for me."

"She's not looking for you. She's found you, and now she's playing some weird game. Why else come to my door?" It hit her suddenly. "Wait, was she the one who left the message?" She'd thought the graffiti odd given Howard's dislike of art.

"It's possible."

She shook her head. "No. No. No. No. I can't have this happening around Annabelle. Do you know what Howard would do if he found out?"

"Annabelle's not in any danger. I'm the one Joella's mad at."

"And you're involved with me. Us." She jabbed herself in the chest. "Who's to say she won't try and hurt me or Annabelle to get to you?"

"I won't allow anything to happen to you."

She noticed how he didn't deny the possibility. "But you can't guarantee that, can you?"

"I'll protect you. I swear."

"The same way you protected me by dumping me?"

He cringed. "I promise, I won't ever leave you again."

"I'm sorry, Gus, but I can't. This isn't just about me being safe, but Annabelle. I can't have her involved in whatever vendetta this woman has going. Not to mention, you killed her brother."

"Not me."

"But you were there. You said you had to stop him."

"Because he was doing horrific things."

"So this takedown you were involved in was a police operation?"

"Not exactly."

Her lips pinched. "Meaning you acted outside the laws, like some kind of vigilante."

"There was no other choice."

"No other choice?" she huffed. "Exactly who are you? The guy I used to know was honest to a fault."

"Still am."

"Are you? Because I get the impression you're hiding something from me."

He sighed and looked to the sky. "I'm not doing it on purpose."

"Then tell me."

"I can't."

"Can't or won't?"

"It's—"

"Complicated?" she interrupted. "That excuse isn't going to fly. I am not a naïve young girl with nothing to lose, Gus. I'm a mother with an impressionable child to take care of, and I won't have you, or anyone for that matter, bringing chaos and violence into her life. She is dealing with enough. We both are."

"What are you saying?" His voice was soft, his expression resigned.

"We can't be involved in whatever trouble

followed you here. I think you need to find somewhere else to stay."

"I'm not even sure it's Joella."

"Doesn't matter. I can't take the chance."

"Lily—"

She closed her eyes and heart against his radiating sadness. "Don't."

"Don't what, love you? Because I do. I never stopped, and seeing you again has made me realize I never will love anyone else."

"I'm sorry, but the answer is still no, and if it helps, you were right to break up with me ten years ago. I don't know who you are anymore, but what I do know is I deserve a life where I'm not afraid."

"I would never hurt you."

"We both know that's a lie because you already have." And with that, she walked away from him, back to her house and her kid sitting on the couch stuffing her face with popcorn. She didn't react as she heard the truck in the driveway rumble to life.

She thought she'd held herself together until Annabelle tucked into her and said softly, "Don't cry, Mommy."

She tried not to. Tried for the sake of her kid. And failed. Her wet pillow in the morning attested to it.

12

The look on Kylie's face killed him.

He'd promised to never hurt her again, and here he was. Doing it again. Not on purpose. But that didn't matter.

She was right. He'd brought danger to her doorstep.

Fucking Joella. Not bad enough she'd fucked over the village she'd ruled over, fucked over the Lycans by helping her brother experiment on them. Now, because she couldn't accept she'd lost, she appeared to have shown up to further fuck with him.

Seriously?

Despite what he'd said to Kylie, he had no doubt it was her. Woman with an eye patch? Sounded about right given the last time he saw her was when one of her brother's creations slashed her face.

What did she want from him?

Revenge seemed most obvious, but why drag Kylie and Annabelle into it?

Unless that was part of her vengeance, to make him lose the one thing he loved.

Unfair. He'd been through so much. Didn't he deserve a second chance?

Kylie had been ready to forgive him. Annabelle willing to accept his presence in their life. He'd had happiness in his grasp, and now he was sitting in his truck, parked outside his old house. A house he'd sold after his brother's death because he'd never planned to return.

Where could he go?

Back to London to see if Brock would take him in? Maybe Ottawa, Canada, where Quinn used to live. That Pack had offered him a chance to join if he needed a place.

But that would be him running away again.

Doing exactly what Kylie accused him of. Leaving.

Never mind the fact she told him to go. She thought he'd take the easy route and flee.

Not this time.

He would show Kylie he could be counted upon, trusted. He would protect her and Annabelle.

With that thought in mind, he left his truck

parked on a side street and hiked back to her house. Would Joella do anything now that he'd left? He didn't know, and he'd not take that chance.

So he waited outside, wondering what they were doing, seeing the glow of lights in the tree placed by the front window and the flash of a television.

Around ten, the place went dark on the main level, but the second floor illuminated. Not the master bedroom, he noticed. She'd gone back to her single bed. The realization took his already crushed heart and wrung it further.

They'd been on the precipice of something beautiful. Her forgiveness leading to the renewal of their love. A love too new and fragile to handle a stress test. And he didn't blame Kylie for that. Given how she'd been hurt before, she had every right to guard herself and the kid.

He dozed for the next two hours, able to sleep just by willing it, a skill learned in the military when you never knew when you'd get your next chance to rest. Just after midnight, he entered the house via the back sliding door. The latch only took a yank to disengage, and it made barely a sound.

He didn't turn on a light. Didn't need to. He might be in his human shape, but he still had excellent night vision. Being restless, he couldn't just sit on the couch playing guard wolf. Luckily, painting didn't make much noise.

He put a thick coat on the hallway walls, and given what she'd said about repainting everything white, proceeded to peel the wallpaper from the living room and kitchen. A part of him knew she'd be pissed in the morning. She'd told him to get out. This was his way of saying that, one, he wasn't going back on his promise to help and, two, he wasn't going anywhere this time, even if it was hard and uncomfortable. She'd accused him before of not trusting her and thinking her too shallow to accept whatever trauma he went through. More like he feared her rejection.

If she knew the real him, would she still love him? So far, it didn't look good. His admission that he'd been involved in a vigilante operation had shocked her. An understandable reaction from someone who hadn't experience violence in her life.

Would she still disagree if she truly knew why he'd had to act?

Joella and her brother had been experimenting on people. Stealing children. Murdering them for their own gain. Would that have changed Kylie's mind if she knew the depth of their depravity?

Maybe, but then he might have had to explain

exactly what kind of experiments. The kind that made men into monsters. Real monsters.

It was funny, because when Gunner first became Lycan, he'd thought himself an unlovable beast. After all, he changed into a wolf under the full moon. He hunted and sometimes even fed in that shape. Conscious the entire time but the primal instinct of the wolf always won over his human qualms.

It took him years to accept he wasn't, in fact, a monster. To realize that Lycans could have a future that involved marriage and family. He just couldn't make any kids. Lycan pregnancies were too dangerous for the mothers. Part of why he'd chosen to split from Kylie. She'd always wanted a few. It was surprising she and Howard stopped at one.

She'd not seemed bothered when he mentioned being sterile. Could she handle knowing every furry detail of why he'd stayed away? Would she better understand if she knew the truth?

What if she hated him for it?

Even if she did hate him, he wouldn't leave her to fend for herself alone. Since he couldn't be sure of Joella's intentions, he had no intention of going anywhere. Since Kylie usually avoided the basement, he chose to hide there as dawn approached. Close by in case Joella tried something but out of sight.

His actions overnight didn't go unnoticed. He heard Kylie as she came down the stairs, the insulation in the basement nonexistent.

"What on earth?" she exclaimed. "Gus, you jerk," was her next huffed declaration.

His phone buzzed in his pocket, and he pulled it free to read her text.

I said go away, not sneak in while I was sleeping and paint my house.

He typed back a reply. *I couldn't leave the job half done.*

I'm changing the locks.

He smirked. *Who says I need a key?*

She stomped into the kitchen, and the water came on as she filled the coffee pot. It took a few minutes for her next message.

I meant what I said. I don't want you coming around.

I am not abandoning you again.

She uttered a cry overheard, and he heard the smash of something hitting and breaking.

He had to forcibly stop himself from racing upstairs. What if she'd cut herself? What if she needed a hug? Someone to hit?

He could just imagine how much she'd freak if she knew he was still in the house. He appeased his conscience by reminding it he only did this to protect her. The moment the danger from Joella was gone, he'd give Kylie the distance she asked for. Even if it killed him. In the meantime, he waited.

She didn't text him back. Understandable. She needed space. Time to process.

Gunner couldn't help himself. He caved and typed a message.

I wouldn't have to sneak in if you gave me permission to paint.

Since you're not living here, I can't afford your services.

He gritted his teeth. *No charge.*

I'm not a charity case.

Never said you were.

Why won't you go away? You're good at that.

Ouch. If accurate. *That was a mistake that I hugely regret. I'm trying to do better.*

Too late.

Not so long as he lived.

He took it as a good sign she kept talking to him. She was right to be angry and afraid. The situation wasn't one most people would know how to handle. But conversation seemed better than the alternative. Her never speaking to him again.

A lighter set of steps arrived down the stairs and a shocked, "Mommy, what happened?

"I dropped my mug. No biggie. It didn't even

have any coffee in it. Now that you're awake, I can run the vacuum."

A bit of banging ensued as Kylie dragged the machine out of a closet, the roar of it loud when it came on. He sat on the washing machine, sending some texts to Brock about the Joella problem, when he heard a gasp. He glanced up to see Annabelle coming down the stairs, holding a box, the one they'd emptied putting up decorations.

She had wide eyes and opened her mouth, but before she could speak, he put a finger to his lips. She got close before dropping her load and whispering, "What are you doing here? I thought you and Mom had a fight."

"We did."

"She cried," the girl declared, giving him a stern look.

"Which was never my intention. I would never hurt Kylie."

"Then why is she mad at you?"

He told her a simple version of the truth. "Because I have enemies."

"That lady who came yesterday?" The kid proved perceptive.

He nodded.

"Why is she your enemy?"

"Her brother did some really bad things, and I helped stop him."

"Because that's what heroes do." Annabelle nodded. "Did you kill him?"

He blinked at the macabre question.

She prodded. "Well, is he dead?"

"Yeah."

"Good."

He arched a brow. "Good?"

Annabelle grinned. "I hate it when heroes let the villains go. It always causes trouble later."

The kid got it. His turn to smile. "Me too."

"Mommy is a softy, though. She won't even kill a spider," Annabelle offered with a disdainful sniff.

"She's always been kind even to gross icky bugs," he agreed.

The vacuum turned off, and Annabelle glanced at the ceiling. "I am pretty sure Mommy loves you. She never looked at Daddy the way she looks at you."

A balm to his aching heart. "And I love her so very, very much, but she's pretty mad at me right now."

"I know. She broke her favorite mug." Said as if it were the most shocking thing ever.

"Any idea how I can fix things with her?"

"It's in too many pieces to glue."

He almost laughed, and yet saw her serious mien. "Maybe I could get her a new one."

"That's a start." Annabelle pursed her lips. "Did you get her a nice present for Christmas?"

"I haven't had time. Any suggestions?"

She tapped her lower lip before confiding, "She loves chocolates with the soft middles."

"Especially the caramel ones." He remembered her picking and choosing when he got her variety boxes.

"Oh, and she really needs a cat."

"A cat?" he couldn't help but query.

Annabelle nodded. "A cat would be cuddly and cute. Everyone loves a cat."

Except for dogs, but he didn't mention that part. "Any idea where I could find one?"

"Mrs. Gertrude up the street in the house with the blue bird mailbox has six kittens. The orange one is the cutest."

"The orange one, eh?"

Annabelle grinned. "He's a boy, and I'll bet he gets to be fat like Garfield.

He almost laughed.

Kylie hollered from upstairs. "You all right down there, Squishy?"

With wide eyes, Annabelle quickly yelled, "All good. Upstairs in a second. I was just looking to see if we missed any Christmas stuff." She then leaned close to murmur, "We're going to the mall so I can buy Daddy a present. We'll be gone for a few hours if you want to paint some more."

"You don't think it will make her madder? She wasn't happy about the hall." He waggled his phone. "She angry-texted me about it."

Annabelle's grin proved infectious as she admitted, "She might pretend to be mad about it, but I saw her staring at it then the walls in the kitchen."

Good to know.

Annabelle left, his co-conspirator in the win-back-Kylie mission. Nice to know he had the kid on his side. Although he had his doubts about the kitten idea for Kylie, but he did need a gift. He'd not seen anything when they went shopping. Chocolates were nice and all, but this was the love of his life. She deserved something special.

A commotion upstairs preceded Kylie and Annabelle leaving the house on foot. Which was when it hit him. She'd said they were going to the mall, and since Kylie didn't have a car...

He could totally set her up with some wheels. The problem being she'd refuse, so he had to figure out how to give one where she couldn't say no. What if it just appeared in her driveway registered in her name? She'd still need insurance. Brock could probably get some set up for her. He had friends all over the place.

It couldn't be anything too new. She'd never accept. But no junkers either because he wouldn't have her breaking down. He thought of that minivan at the garage. Easy to buy. He just needed a way to give it to her.

The commotion upstairs ended in the front door being shut as they left. With them gone, he returned to the main floor and debated. Following them would get him in trouble if Kylie spotted him. Not following them meant hoping Joella didn't try anything in public.

A woman with an eyepatch would be pretty noticeable, but nothing would prevent her from hiring goons.

Fuck.

He hurried outside in time to see the bus pulling away. He might have worried about them even making it aboard, but Annabelle peeked out the rear window and must have seen him, because she waved.

No one would try anything with that many witnesses, and he had time before they reached the mall. Time enough for him to secure her house, which he should have done the night before when they found the message. He'd been so sure it was her ex. In retrospect, he could kick himself for being an idiot.

He started by checking every single window was locked. He already knew the back door into the yard was an issue. The sliding glass door with its flimsy latch was too easy to pop. He cut a piece of wood to fit in the frame so that when it was closed, no one could force it open. Breaking glass would give some warning. The basement windows were too small unless Joella resorted to super-scrawny thugs. Even Joella herself wouldn't likely fit.

The front door had a lock that would be easy to pick. He couldn't exactly change it without Kylie noticing, given she'd need a new key, not to mention it would be hard to miss shiny new brass versus old and tarnished.

Instead, he wrangled a bell over it that would jangle each time it opened and which Kylie might very well rip down. As he did so, a car slowed down in front of her place, an older sedan, the windows dark and tinted.

It stopped, and a guy got out, not very tall, maybe five ten, but with a stocky build. His dark hair had been shaved to the skin on the sides, revealing the ink that stretched from his scalp down his neck. The tattooed dude strode to the front door and rapped hard on it.

It occurred to Gunner to pretend no one was home to see what happened, but his curiosity about the stranger won. Gunner swung open the portal. "Hey. Can I help you?"

"I'm looking for the lady of the house."

"She's unavailable. Maybe I can help."

"When will she back?"

"That's none of your business. And I'm going to add I'm pretty sure she doesn't have anything to talk to you about."

The fellow scowled. "We're looking for her husband."

"You mean ex-husband," Gunner clarified even as he wondered what business Keeler would have with this kind of lowlife. They say you shouldn't judge a person by their appearance, but a guy who tattooed his face with Fuck You and a middle finger, yeah, not exactly a model citizen.

"Whatever. We know she lives here with his kid. She needs to tell us where the fucker's hiding."

"Have you checked his house?"

"Do I look stupid?" the guy growled.

"Actually, if I'm being honest..." He taunted, and the fellow rose to the bait.

The thug swung.

Gunner caught the fist and tsked. "Now, that's

not very nice and only days before Christmas. What would Santa say?"

"You're messing with the wrong guy." Tattoo dude tugged and only embarrassed himself further when he couldn't get free.

"I couldn't have said it better. I am not someone you want to piss off." Gunner remained pleasant and smiling.

It caused tattoo guy to bluster. "Listen, motherfucker, our beef ain't with you or Howard's ex. We just want to collect the money he owes us."

"Oh, do tell me more."

"I ain't telling you shit."

"Wrong answer." Gunner yanked him inside and closed the door, shoving him up against the wall, inwardly cringing since he'd probably scuffed the new paint.

"Let me go."

"Nope." Gunner lifted him higher. "Here's the deal, dickweed—you don't mind if I call you dickweed? After all it's not like you introduced your rude ass. You don't get to show up here being all threatening and stuff. There's a child in this house. A child and a mother I'm rather fond of. So as you can imagine, I don't really appreciate you showing up here, causing trouble when it's Howard that's the problem."

"You're messing with the wrong—"

Gunner pulled him forward and slammed tattoo dude hard enough his eyes rolled. He got close as he growled, "Wrong. I am the one you should be worried about, because do you know what happens to people I don't like? They go missing. As in never found again. Because I'm not one to fuck around with assholes. And you are an asshole."

The door shoved open suddenly as his companion came inside to check on his partner, but Gunner had been expecting it. He kicked out his foot and caught the new guy in the knee, hitting it hard enough it twisted unnaturally. The big fellow crumpled with a cry of pain. Gunner then clocked the one he held a few times, dazing him before grabbing the head of the big one and kneeing him in the face until he heard a crunch.

Only when both of them were on the floor, holding their faces, with the bigger one whimpering, did Gunner address them.

"Who sent you?"

"Our boss," the big guy said, holding his face.

"Who is your boss? Is it a woman with an eyepatch?" Had Joella sent them?

Tattoo dude scoffed. "We ain't working for no woman pirate. But when our boss hears what happened, he's gonna fuck you up good. You and your bitch."

Wrong thing to say. Gunner released some pent-up frustration on the thugs, his anger landing his blows, his instincts blocking their feeble attempts. Only when they were bleeding, sniveling messes on the floor at his feet did he address them.

"So here's what's going to happen, dickwads. You're going to forget this address. You're going to leave and never return. As a matter of fact, you'll avoid this street. Because if catch you anywhere near Keeler's ex-wife or kid, I will fucking kill you. Slowly. And painfully."

"Why don't you tell our boss? He's the one who wants Howard to pay," complained the tattoo dude.

"Sounds like that's between your boss and Howard. If it helps, I don't care what you do to him. But whatever you do happens elsewhere. Not here. Not near his ex or the kid. Do I make myself clear?"

The first guy glared, making it obvious he had issues still. Gunner's next blow didn't hold back.

Through the broken front teeth in his mouth, the guy managed a garbled, "Ash-hool."

The big dude got the message, though. "We won't mess with your woman. Let's go." He supported the other thug out the door and into the car. It sped off, and Gunner pursed his lips.

What had Howard gotten himself into? And would he have to fix it? Because here was the thing, much as he hated the guy, and he doubted Kylie would miss him, there was a little girl out there who loved her daddy.

Still, this kind of bullshit couldn't be allowed. Imagine if Kylie had been home.

Time to pay Howard another visit. As if he didn't have enough on his plate. First, he cleaned up all signs of the fight, the blood on the floor nasty. He then did a quick coat of paint on the hall, the second coat hiding the scuff from where he'd shoved the thug. He even did a few swipes on the walls he'd stripped overnight.

Only then did he leave, locking the door behind him.

Where oh where could Howard, who owed money to the wrong kind of people, be hiding? He fired off a text to Brock. *Need a favor. Can you ping the last location for this phone number?* He entered Howard's cell.

It took his friend under five minutes to post a reply.

Keeler Winery. Howard went to work. Not hiding at all. Just dumb fucking thugs who'd obviously thought they could leverage Kylie and Annabelle to get him to pay.

Gunner paid a visit the winery and was sipping a glass of something nice in the reception area when the man himself appeared.

"What are you doing here?" Howard snarked.

"You and I need to talk about your debt problem."

"I don't know what you're talking about."

"Two rough-looking guys came by Kylie's place looking for you. Said you owed them money."

He blanched. "Are they okay?"

"Luckily, they weren't home, and I had a chat with them about showing up in the future. Care to explain what the fuck that was about?"

For a moment, the brash man had a haughty expression. Then his shoulders sagged. "I'm in trouble."

Gunner poured himself another glass then one for Howard. "Sit down and tell me about it."

With a sigh, Howard unburdened himself. As with many rich men, he'd decided to gamble with money he didn't have.

Howard gestured as he tried to justify his actions. "I was on a winning streak. It should have been a sure-fire bet."

Gunner snorted. "Which is how they get you each time. How much do you owe?"

"Almost a million." A soft, shamed admission.

He whistled. "That's a lot of cash."

"I know, which is why I told them I'd need a bit of time to gather it."

"Let me guess, they got impatient."

Howard nodded.

"You do realize they won't give up. If you don't pay them, they will hurt someone. It's what those types of people do."

"I know, and I should have it soon." Howard ducked his head. "I guess you're going to tell Kylie so she can use it against me."

It hadn't even occurred to Gunner. Snitches get stitches. However, he shouldn't let Howard completely off the hook. "Actually, I won't say anything if you help me with something."

"What?"

Once he and Howard hammered out the details, he left and headed for the mall. He parked a short distance from the bus stop and then waited since her cell phone showed her still inside.

He spotted them the moment they emerged, headed for the bus stop, smiling as they swung their shopping bags.

A bus that wouldn't be coming since the driver suddenly got a text from dispatch telling him to put his vehicle out of service. Wouldn't the maintenance crew be confused when he suddenly showed up?

Not his problem.

As Kylie checked her phone and frowned, Gunner stopped in front of them. He rolled down his window and tossed a casual, "Hey, need a ride home?"

He could see Kylie wanted to say no, but a light snow had begun to fall, and the next bus wasn't expected for at least thirty minutes. But what cinched it?

Annabelle hopped right on in with her bags and heaved a relieved sigh as she said, "Thank you for saving us! I was not looking forward to that smelly bus ride home."

13

Kylie didn't believe for one minute that Gunner just happened to drive by. It was too coincidental for her liking. However, Annabelle didn't have a problem with piling in and perching on that middle seat, and honestly, Kylie wasn't in the mood to wait who knew how long for the next bus.

The old-style truck had a front seat bench that could seat three. She squeezed in beside Annabelle, stowing the bags at her feet since the truck had no backseat.

Her daughter giggled as she stated, "Now I'm a real squishy!"

"But much cuter than the toy kind," Kylie added.

"Well duh, I'm super adorbs," Annabelle replied, giving her hair a flick.

Gunner chuckled. "You remind me so much of your mom when she was a kid."

"Annabelle is much smarter, though." Kylie spent the time with her reading and practicing math that her parents never did.

Gunner pulled away from the curb. "Have you guys had supper yet?"

"No, but I'll make something quick when we get home," Kylie quickly answered.

Annabelle's lips turned down. "Meaning soup. Blech. It's not food if you can suck it through a straw."

The sassy reply had Kylie biting her lower lip, but Gunner outright laughed. "I don't suppose I could convince you to maybe share a bucket of crispy fried chicken and taters?"

"We really shouldn't," Kylie murmured, but Annabelle bounced.

"Please, Mommy. You know I love crunchy chicken!"

If it were just her, she'd had said no out of spite, but she wasn't about to let her annoyance with Gunner ruin her daughter's smile. "I guess. But only if you promise to have a few bites of coleslaw." Which counted as a vegetable, right?

"Yay!" Sung not just by Annabelle but Gunner too.

They hit a finger-licking good location drive-thru, which had a small lineup, not that it bothered the two peas in a pod as they discussed the merits of the various chicken chains.

Gunner paid for the meal, and Kylie knew better than to offer to help. He remained very alpha male in that respect, and besides, she'd already spent enough today. Pretending to use the washroom while Annabelle ate her cinnamon-sprinkled, freshly made donut in the food court, she'd run to a store to get the newest video game. She just hoped Howard hadn't gotten her the same one. Then again, he rarely paid attention to gifts, usually trusting those purchases to Kylie. She wondered if his new girlfriend had helped or if he'd had to shop on his own.

The food did smell awfully good, and the ride home was luckily short, given they could drive directly there instead of making a zillion stops on the bus. Her place looked Christmassy with the lightly falling snow and the lights twinkling.

As they walked in, Gunner did caution, "I put a final coat of paint in the hall so you might want to be careful touching the walls. They might still be sticky."

She shot him an annoyed look over Annabelle's head. So much for his listening to her when she said to go away.

He shrugged and grinned, completely unrepentant.

As for Annabelle, she didn't seem bothered at all as she clapped her hands. "This house is starting to look more and more like home. I can't wait until we do the living room and get rid of those ugly curtains."

Those ugly curtains had taken several washes to rinse them of the nicotine stench. But Annabelle had a point. Imagine the white walls offset by some nice sheer drapes, maybe in a light blue. It would look nice with the navy-blue couch, the one thing she'd splurged on when they moved in since the old plaid thing not only stank it reminded her too much of her mom.

As Annabelle carried their meal to the kitchen, Kylie moved close enough to Gunner to hiss, "I told you to stay away."

"And I told you I ain't running this time."

"It's not running if I kick you out."

"You told me to be honest, so I was."

"About your war trauma. Not the fact you're basically a criminal."

"I assure you no one is going to arrest me for anything I've done."

She glared at him. "Is that supposed to make me feel better?"

"I'm going to guess by your tone and expression it doesn't."

She jabbed him in the chest with her finger. "I won't have you putting my child in danger."

"And you obviously don't know me very well if you think I'd ever let anything happen to either of you."

She might have said more, but Annabelle hollered from the kitchen, "You guys coming to eat? Because I am hungry enough there might not be any leftovers."

"We're coming," he yelled.

We. He kept talking and acting as if this were just a disagreement. Kept speaking as if he wouldn't budge.

She wanted to blast him and toss him out on his ear. At the same time, the fact he refused to leave did much to ease her annoyance. Did she really expect a man who'd gone to fight for his country would come back the same? He'd always had a strong, altruistic streak. Was it so crazy to imagine that he might not be the type of person who would sit back if he saw something wrong happening?

She read in the news just about every day about injustices and how the law failed to protect. Did it make him a bad person because he wasn't content to sit back and let evil run unchecked?

Dinner proved enjoyable, even if Kylie didn't say too much. She didn't have to because she absorbed her daughter and Gunner hitting it off as if they'd known each other forever. For a kid not born of his loins, they shared many traits beyond loving ice cream and crunchy chicken.

No gravy, ketchup for dipping all the way. The knock-knock jokes they traded were eye-roll worthy. They even offered to clean up together, with Annabelle washing while he dried, chatting away with an ease Kylie envied.

Annabelle didn't bring a ton of baggage and hurt into the equation. She saw and liked Gunner for who he was. Or at least appeared to be.

But he still had secrets, meaning he'd not been completely truthful with her. The question being, what kind? She liked to think she'd been honest with him, but at the same time, she had held some of herself back.

Like the fact she'd been happy with Howard in the beginning. He'd been courteous during her pregnancy. While not the most helpful dad with a newborn, he'd hired someone to handle the cooking and cleaning until Kylie insisted on taking it over herself when Annabelle transitioned past the extremely needy stage of babyhood. He'd taken her on date nights. Never forgot her birthday or anniversary. Bought her nice gifts. Didn't cheat.

Yet she never really loved him, and over time, he came to sense that. Or so she assumed given how he changed around her. He became more critical. Less attentive. The sex went from not often to rare to not happening. Not because he didn't want it but because she had no desire for him.

In many respects, the divorce wasn't his fault, but hers, because she wanted more out of a relationship. No, that wasn't accurate. She wanted someone else. The person who used to make her whole.

And now he was in her kitchen, flicking suds at Annabelle, who laughed and snapped him with her towel. A girl who loved her dad but had enough affection to accept another.

The question was, could Kylie? Part of the reason why she'd tried to make Gunner leave was because he gave her a convenient excuse. And she jumped on it, seized it, and made it into a big deal because, deep down, she was terrified he'd hurt her again.

What would happen if she allowed herself to love him? A love that had never truly gone away. What if she threw herself into a relationship with him and he left her?

I would survive. After all, she'd done it once

before. It hurt. It devastated. But the world didn't end. It moved on and simply became different.

"Your mom is looking way too serious," Gunner teased as he entered the living room, Squishy at his heels.

"That's her 'I'm making big decisions' face," Annabelle confided.

"Haha, you two." Kylie softened her retort with a smile. "I was just thinking with the weather being terrible, maybe Gunner should spend the night." The snow falling outside had thickened, but that proved only to be a convenient excuse. She didn't want him to go.

His jaw dropped in surprise, but he quickly recovered and grinned. "That would be awesome. I could get going on some more paint."

"Or you could wait until the morning and join us for a movie. Tonight's pre-Christmas special is..." She glanced at Annabelle, who beamed from ear to ear.

"The Nightmare Before Christmas."

His brows rose. "Don't tell me your mom convinced you it was a Christmas movie?"

"It's got Santa and presents," was Kylie's pert reply. They used to argue about it every year as kids. But every year he watched it with her.

"Fine. But just so you know, I will expect to see

Hans Gruber fall off the Nakatomi building before Christmas Day."

"Oh god, no," Kylie moaned.

Whereas Annabelle giggled. "Now you sound like my dad. We watch it every Christmas Eve."

"Sounds like your dad's got good taste." Gunner's gaze met hers over Annabelle's head.

She couldn't hold it and ducked her chin. "All right, you two, let's get this movie marathon going. I'd like to squeeze in *Santa Versus the Snowman* after Jack saves the day."

"Saves? Ha. It's his fault Christmas almost gets ruined," Gunner insisted.

"But only because he's misunderstood," Kylie argued.

To which Annabelle chimed in, "Shh, it's starting."

Despite Annabelle sitting between them, it proved to be an intimate evening. Every time Kylie happened to glance sideways, Gunner met her gaze.

Around ten, Kylie sent Annabelle to bed while he remained on the couch. She returned to find him in the front window, looking grim.

"Something wrong?" she asked.

"No, but I need to tell you something."

"Oh."

"This afternoon, while you were gone, some goons came by your house."

She blinked. That wasn't what she expected to hear. "Excuse me?"

"Don't worry. I sent them on their way."

"You promised you wouldn't put us in danger," she hissed, suddenly regretting her invitation to stay.

"They weren't here for me, and I debated telling you, especially since I kind of swore I wouldn't. But for the sake of honesty, and for you to be vigilant, you needed to know."

"Are you saying they were here for me?" She couldn't fathom why.

"Not you. Your ex got himself into a bit of trouble gambling."

"That can't be right. Howard doesn't gamble."

"With good reason since he sucks at it. Apparently, he owes a tidy sum of cash to unsavory sorts."

"And they came here looking for it from me?" she squeaked.

He nodded. "Don't worry. I handled it and made it clear that they weren't to bother you or Annabelle."

"What about Howard?"

He shrugged. "The man owes them money. The best I could do was talk to Keeler and tell him what happened."

"Wait, you went to see Howard?"

"Yeah. How do you think I knew about the debt? Anyhow, he said he'd take care of it, but I thought you should know in case those thugs came around again. If I'm not here, don't answer the door and call me right away."

"Shouldn't I call 911?"

"I'll be faster."

She hugged herself as she paced. "Do you think they'll be back?"

"They'd be stupid to, given I made my warning to them quite clear."

She paused to eye him. "Do I want to know what that means?"

"Probably not."

A heavy breath huffed from her. "Seriously? As if I didn't have enough to deal with."

"Nothing will happen to you or Annabelle."

She closed her eyes as she tried to not imagine what could have happened had she been home instead. Would these ruffians have taken them hostage against Howard? Or did that only happen in the movies?

"I'm going to murder Howard myself," she grumbled.

"No, you're not, because you're not supposed to know. I swore I wouldn't tell you."

"You can't be serious?" She eyed him.

"Give him a chance to make it right."

"You're taking his side?"

"No, but let's be honest, what good will come from confronting him over it? It's almost Christmas. Pretty sure you don't want Annabelle to be stuck in the middle of a fight."

She pursed her lips. He had a point. But that didn't mean she'd forget. If Howard started pulling his stunts with custody again, she would use it. "Any other things I should know?" A sour query.

"Well, I was gonna wait to tell you this, but in the spirit of coming completely clean, there is one more big secret left. I'm a werewolf."

She snorted. "Now is not the time for jokes."

"Not kidding." He sighed. "Remember how I said I came back from the military changed? It's because, when I was a prisoner, I got bitten by a Lycan, which is what werewolves like to call themselves. That chomp changed me into one. It's why I can't have kids. Why I basically went on a decade-long woe-is-me tantrum."

She stared at him. "This isn't funny."

"No, it's not, but it is the truth. And not something you can tell anyone. The Cabal has very strict rules about this."

"The Cabal?"

"The group governing Lycans around the world."

"Because there's enough werewolves that they need a group to keep them in line, or is that on a leash?" She uttered a short laugh. "Wow. I can see why the military discharged you if you're going around claiming to be a werewolf."

"It's the truth," he insisted.

"Then show me."

"I can't, not without a full moon."

That brought another snort. "Of course. So you're telling me on Christmas Day you're going to suddenly turn into a howling, hairy beast? And then what? You'll maul me? Gonna eat the neighbor?"

"Now you're being dramatic. Yes, I sometimes hunt in that form, but things like rabbits or deer."

She rubbed her face. "I'm too tired to play games with you, Gunner."

"You asked me what I was hiding. That's it. That's my secret. My reason for not coming back. I thought if you knew, you'd hate me. That you'd see me as a monster."

She looked at him, a man with a stubble on his jaw, looking utterly serious, and handsome, completely delusional, but not through any fault of his own. His experiences in the military had changed him. But the good man she knew remained. A man who needed understanding and compassion—and a shrink.

She held out her hand. "Let's go to bed."

"Aren't you going to ask questions?"

"Not tonight. How about I save them for after the full moon?"

His lips quirked. "You don't believe me."

"I believe that you believe."

His head shook. "Okay. But I want it known I tried to warn you."

"Noted. Now, bed? We have a busy day tomorrow."

"Oh? What are we doing?"

"We are going to be building the biggest snowman followed by a snow fort while guzzling mushmallow-topped hot chocolate—"

"Mushmallow?"

"I'll let Annabelle explain it."

"What about the painting?"

"Save it for when Annabelle's at her dad's." She grabbed him by the hand, a part of her worried that she was making the wrong choice, but a larger part of her wanted to take this chance with the man she'd always loved.

"I love you, Lily."

She cast a coy glance over her shoulder as she replied, "Show me."

He wasted no time. He carried her up the stairs to the master bedroom, closing the door quietly, a reminder that tonight they weren't alone.

Having to be quiet added an element of the forbidden to their lovemaking. He was ardent and attentive. She tried to not cry out by shoving her fist in her mouth. When his body covered hers and he thrust into her, her lips clung to the flesh of his shoulder to stifle her gasps. When she came, she accidentally bit him. He grunted and stilled inside her, his shaft pulsing, his body trembling.

And when he looked down into her eyes, he smiled as he murmured, "I am so happy you're mine."

She dragged him down for a kiss, and when it came time for orgasm number two, he was the one who couldn't contain himself and nipped her.

They slept intertwined. Moving past the hurt. Getting to the truth. Becoming stronger for it.

When Kylie got caught by her daughter in the hall the next morning, wearing just her sweater since she had no clothes in the room, she smiled as Annabelle said, "I'm glad you and Gunner made up."

Me too.

14

Gunner couldn't believe how well the previous night had gone. He'd told Kylie the truth, and while he could see she didn't believe him, she hadn't turned away or tossed him out. He could understand her skepticism, but soon she'd meet his wolf, which would be the true test.

He had to admit to being nervous. What if it was too much for her to handle? What if she never looked at him again with love in her eyes?

He might never recover. But he'd deal with that if it happened. *If* being the keyword. For a decade, he'd been psyching himself out, convinced no one could love him. Letting go of that fear proved hard, but the reward if it went well meant being with the woman he'd always loved and gaining a daughter.

Fuck, he hoped the truth didn't ruin everything,

because, now that he'd gotten a taste of belonging, he wanted it more than ever.

He handled the bacon portion of breakfast while Annabelle made the pancakes. Kylie was in charge of coffee and whipped cream. All kinds of fuel to get them ready for the snow day, which began with him shoveling the walkway with help. Annabelle grabbed a second shovel, and together they worked on it while Kylie tossed snowballs until they ganged up on her. Then it was snowman time, with Annabelle cackling like a fiend as Gunner bulked up the stick arms with snow to simulate muscle. Kylie provided a wood spoon for a nose.

The fort ended up more like two ditches that they hid behind to have a snowball fight. Then they chased the chill with hot chocolate topped with mushmallows, which he agreed was a much better name.

It was the most perfect day ever.

Later that afternoon, he got a phone call from an unknown number. He answered, mostly because he loved fucking with scammers. The girls were busy trying to street fight in some video game with Kylie mashing buttons and hooting every time she flattened Annabelle's fighter with the bull head.

He stepped into the kitchen as he said, "Yeah.

"Happy almost Christmas," exclaimed Quinn.

That was a surprise. "What is it with you and Brock being all chatty on the phone lately?" he grumbled good-naturedly.

"It occurs to me that I should have done better about keeping in touch. So, hey. How's it going?"

A glance in the living room had him saying an honest, "Good, real good. You?"

"Never better."

"You and the doc somewhere safe?" he asked. Last time he'd seen Quinn and Dr. Erryn Silver in Romania, they'd had to flee and go into hiding since the Cabal wanted to bring them in for questioning. Also known as "getting rid of loose ends."

"No need. Not since Brock joined the team. With Dmitri gone and the truth now out there, we're no longer being hunted," Quinn explained.

"Damn, that's awesome, bro." Gunner was happy for his friend.

"No shit. It means the research doc is doing won't get buried. A good thing since it's been eye-opening."

"You figured out yet why Sascha was so interested in the Lycan-born females?" The mad scientist had been kidnapping and using them to fuel his experiments.

"Starting to. Doc already knew there was something in her saliva that brings out the Lycan even if there's no full moon. It can even turn humans if concentrated enough, which explains that old boyfriend of hers that turned and mauled her."

Gunner whistled. "Damn, that's wild. No wonder the Cabal wanted to keep her under wraps."

"That's not even the half of it, bro. In my case, since we're mated, her kisses literally make me stronger. Just need a cape and I could be a superhero."

"No cape."

"You and Doc, ruining all my fun," Quinn grumbled.

"I'm okay with that," was Gunner's dry reply.

"Then there's her blood, which reverses a shift, which will be useful if we can find a way to synthesize it. It would mean no more worrying about shifting on full moons. Possibly even a cure someday. Not that I'd want it but thought you might want to know."

There was a time Gunner would have done anything to not be Lycan. Now? "We'll see. Life's pretty good these days."

"Glad to hear it, bro, and hate what I gotta say next."

His stomach clenched. "What's wrong?"

"I've got it on good authority Joella is looking for you."

"I know."

"You've seen her?"

"Not exactly." He told Quinn what had happened thus far, and his friend whistled.

"Be careful. We don't know what she's capable of. We assumed Sascha's bullshit experiments stopped when he died, but for all we know, he's got more secret labs and stashes of monsters somewhere else."

"Shit, I'd not even thought of that." He rubbed his face.

"Do me a favor and sit tight. Would have been there already if not for the snow."

"Wait, you're coming here?" He couldn't stem his surprise.

"Yeah, was gonna surprise you, but given the cancellation of our flight, not sure when we'll make it."

"Dude." That was all he could say as his throat tightened.

"Do me a favor and stay out of trouble until we get there."

"Silver's coming with you?"

"And Brock. You'll get to meet his vampire princess."

"Shit. You guys are really worried."

Quinn's voice lowered to a somber tone. "We

failed to be there for you once before. it won't happen again."

He hung up feeling tight inside. Kylie neared and put a hand on him. "You okay, Gus?"

"Yeah." A whispered word. "Finally feeling like everything's going to be all right."

The moment he said it, he wanted to take it back. Talk about trying to jinx it.

Kylie wrapped her arms around him. "I sure hope so."

The rest of the day went well. They had tacos for dinner and then watched *Frosty*, the original cartoon classic, which did involve singing. If his army buddies ever saw it, they would have laughed and called him names.

When Annabelle went to bed, he helped Kylie wrap some presents for the kid and told her he planned to pick up some skates and a toboggan.

Apparently, that was code for passionate sex because she mauled him on the living room floor. Not that he complained.

Howard's arrival the next morning didn't ruin his happy glow. How could it? He'd spent the night in Kylie's arms.

What did bother him? The sad expression on her face as she watched from the door as Annabelle left with her dad to spend Christmas at his parents' place.

Gunner put an arm around her shoulder. She turned into him, and he held her as she cried.

Not for long. She soon wiped her eyes and offered a husky, "What do you say we get dirty painting so we can have an excuse to shower?"

Fuck, yeah.

He did his best to keep her spirits bright, blasting Christmas tunes as they slathered a white coat on every wall he'd prepped, including the bedroom. They had a candlelight dinner of Chinese food with some wine that he'd bought.

As she snuggled against him, watching the fireplace channel on television, she murmured, "Tomorrow's the big day."

He thought she meant Christmas and replied, "No presents for you until morning."

She snorted. "I'm a little old to care about that. I meant the wolf thing. You said it happens on the full moon."

"It does. For me, since I am not an alpha, it requires moonlight to touch my skin. The more skin exposed, the quicker the transition."

"What happens if you're out in public and it happens?"

"For one, Lycans know better than to be far from a safe place on a full moon."

"A safe place being..."

"Some will draw the curtains and blinds or lock themselves in a windowless room to avoid it. Wolfsbane can also help, but given its poisonous attributes, it's not recommended."

"So do you bust out of your clothes when it happens? Does it hurt?"

"I strip beforehand. Usually, I'll find myself a place to park by some woods. Somewhere a wolf won't seem out of place."

"Aren't you worried about hunters?" She asked serious questions.

"Yup. Bullets hurt."

"I thought only silver killed a werewolf?"

"Nah, any kind of bullet to the head or through the heart will do it. But I will note we are tougher than most. We heal faster. We're stronger, too, with heightened senses."

"Oh?" She tilted her head to see his face. "So you're like a superhero."

He snorted. "Nope. Just a guy who turns into a wolf on the full moon."

"Who takes care of bad guys."

"Again, not entirely accurate. I went after Sascha and his gang because they were harming Lycans like me. If you're worried I'm going to start roaming the streets of town, getting rid of criminals, don't. I have no plans to draw attention to myself."

"What if this Joella person comes after you, though?"

"Then I'll handle it."

"Going to bite her face off?" she joked, drinking her wine.

"Only if she's dumb enough to come at me on the full moon."

She sounded entirely sober as she said, "You really believe all this, don't you?"

"Crazy as it sounds, it's true. I just hope once you realize it that you'll still look at me the same."

She shifted to straddle his lap. "I love you. Even if you do think you're a werewolf." Her lips quirked as she grabbed his cock and said, "Ready to howl?"

He did more than howl as she rode him, her head tilted back, her hips rotating and grinding as she set the tempo.

Eventually they made it to bed, and when they woke the next morning, he murmured, "Merry Christmas, Lily."

The first of many, he hoped.

15

Christmas morning and Kylie didn't want to get up, not with her heart so heavy. Bless Gunner's sweet heart, he tried. He insisted she stay in bed and brought her breakfast: an omelet with ham and cheese, coffee with some Bailey's Irish Cream, and fresh-cut fruit.

He ran her a hot bath with bubbles. When she initiated sex, he made it all about her pleasure, going down on her for so long she came twice.

Eventually, she could avoid the real world no longer and went downstairs. She immediately saw the tree with Annabelle's presents underneath. She couldn't help a sniffle.

Gunner put his arm around her shoulders. "Don't cry, Lily. I know it's hard. Maybe I can help.

Sit." He gently guided her to the couch. "Why don't you open your gifts?"

"But I didn't get you anything," she wailed. Tight budget and their fight meant she'd not expected to spend Christmas morning with him.

"You gave me the only thing I ever wanted. A second chance."

She blinked back tears. "You're being too nice."

"More like I've got ten years of spoiling you to catch up on," was his grinned reply. "Now get ready to tear some paper."

It started with a box of filled chocolates, followed by a silky set of pajamas. However, it was the manila envelope he handed her that puzzled.

She eyed it then him. "What's this?"

"Open it and see."

She tore it open and stared at the schematics he'd printed off. She had to read the title of the plans twice before her mouth rounded. "Is this a blueprint design for a treehouse?"

"Yup. Our special tree has gotten bigger since I built the last one, and it occurs to me that Annabelle would like—"

He never finished his sentence, as she threw herself at him. "Thank you. Thank you." She smothered him in kisses, and he laughed.

"I haven't even built it yet."

"I don't care. I love it. I love you!" The fact he'd even thought of it had her feeling less morose.

"You think she'll like it?" He actually sounded worried.

"Are you kidding?" Kylie exclaimed. "She saw a few leftover boards in the tree and wouldn't stop asking me about it. She's going to be over the moon."

"Sweet. We obviously won't be able to build until spring, but I figured it would give us time to modify it to suit her personality."

"Anyone ever tell you how amazing you are?"

His lips twisted. "Amazing would have been me manning up a decade ago, but at the same time, if I had, we wouldn't have an amazing kid."

Put that way, it was hard to regret how life turned out because she wouldn't trade her Squishy for anything in the world.

Since Kylie had nothing to give Gunner, she gave him the one thing she could. An epic blowjob, which had him gasping for air.

Around lunch time, he slapped her on the butt and said, "Get dressed."

"Why?" she moaned. She rather enjoyed the way he couldn't stop staring as she walked around in his shirt and nothing else.

"Trust me. I have a surprise for you."

Apparently, it wasn't the nachos he whipped

together using the leftovers from taco night. As the hour approached one, he kept glancing at his watch.

"Expecting someone?" she asked.

"Yup." His head turned as if he had X-ray vision and could see through the walls. "And they're here."

"Who?"

"Go see," he urged, pushing her out of the kitchen.

Bemused, she had to wonder who he'd invited. She had no family other than—

Annabelle walked in wearing her Christmas hat, yodeling a cheery, "Merry Christmas!"

"Squishy!" Kylie screamed as she threw herself at her daughter, hugging her tight. "What are you doing here?"

"Daddy brought me." Annabelle glanced over her shoulder, and Kylie looked out to see Howard standing there, wearing an overcoat and a hat that Annabelle had to have chosen since it had the Grinch on it.

"Thank you," she said.

Her ex sighed. "Actually, thank Gunner. He talked me into doing the right thing even if it did piss off my parents. But it's only for a few hours. I promised to bring her back for dinner."

"Yay!" Kylie squealed. She turned a bright smile on Gunner. "Best present ever."

He winked. "I had some help from a great dad."

A claim that had Howard shifting as if uncomfortable.

Kylie practically dragged Annabelle inside. "Let's get you opening presents."

Squishy giggled. "Give me a second. I gotta go pee."

Her kid went off, and Kylie hung up her coat, pausing as she heard the murmur of male voices. Gunner had stepped outside to talk to Howard, and while it might be wrong, she listened.

"Really appreciate you bringing the kid over," Gunner said.

"Much as I'd like to be a dick about it, Annabelle's needs are more important than me being petty."

The remark had Gunner chuckling. "Doing the right thing is harder than they tell you."

"You don't say."

"What of that problem we discussed? Did you handle it yet?"

Kylie held her breath. She could only assume Gunner referenced the secret he'd told her about.

Howard's tone dropped an octave. "I am heading there now to deal with it. The bookie wasn't happy with how badly you messed up his goons, though."

"Then they shouldn't have tried to drag Kylie

and Annabelle into it." Gunner's firm tone sent a shiver down her spine.

"I appreciate the fact you've got my kid's back."

To her surprise, Gunner said, "Yours, too, if you ever need it. A girl shouldn't be without her father."

"Well, here's to hoping I don't ever have to take you up on that offer. This was a sobering lesson. Never gambling again," Howard swore.

"Don't say never. I might want to occasionally fleece you at poker for shits and giggles."

Howard chuckled. "The only thing I'm wagering from now on is cases of beer like we used to do in college."

"Sounds good to me. Merry Christmas, Keeler."

"Merry Christmas, Hendry."

Kylie scooted from the door before Gunner caught her snooping. She'd just flopped on the couch when Annabelle came flying in.

"Present time!" she chirped.

Paper flew and excited chatter abounded as Annabelle exclaimed over every single gift, declaring it perfect, from the video game to the makeup kit to the tickets to see Monster Trucks from Gunner.

Monster Trucks? she'd mouthed in surprise in Gunner's direction.

He winked at the time but later whispered to her, "Figured since you and Howard had the artsy stuff covered, I'd introduce her to some different kind of stuff."

Which probably also explained the sling shot. But he didn't only get her traditionally masculine things, he also brought up from the basement a giant stuffed pink unicorn that had Annabelle laughing as she threw herself on it. "It's so fluffy!"

But it was when he showed her the plans for the tree house and offered to let her help that Annabelle hugged him tight. "Thanks."

"Bah. It's nothing."

Annabelle glanced at a teary-eyed Kylie and shook her head. "It's everything." Then in a rare moment of candor, her kid said, "You know how to make Mommy happy."

He truly did.

All too soon, Howard returned to take Annabelle, and while it was hard watching her go, she didn't say a disparaging word but waved from the front step until they drove out of sight.

The sky turned overcast, the clouds getting heavy with more snow.

Remembering their conversation of the night before, she teased Gunner. "Uh-oh. Guess the wolf show is going to get postponed for bad weather."

He eyed the sky. "No. It'll be a bit harder, but

not impossible. Even if the moon is hidden, it's up there."

"So how long before the striptease? Aren't you worried you'll get frostbite on your manparts?"

"My manparts will be fine," he snorted.

"If you say so. It would be a shame if something happened to them," she murmured, turning into his arms.

"One thing I should warn is if I change, I most likely won't be able to turn back until morning."

"If this is your way of saying we're doing it doggy style, I am going to have to decline. No dogs on my bed."

He outright laughed. "I can't believe you said that, and, no, we won't be having sex. I know some dudes think it's okay and their mates are all right with it, but I am totally not."

"So these werewolf friends of yours are married?"

"Yup. As a matter of fact, you'll meet them soon. They're supposed to be showing up anytime now. Brock's bringing his girlfriend from London, and Quinn's hitched to a doctor."

Had he found himself some delusional friends, or did they play along with his mental trauma? Perhaps, with time and love, he'd heal enough to decipher the difference between fantasy and reality.

"What do you want for dinner?" she asked. "I could whip up a pasta casserole." Not exactly the traditional turkey, but better than her original plan of gorging on ice cream.

"Not really hungry after that afternoon snack," he said, rubbing his tummy. She and Annabelle had whipped up some Rice Krispies squares with chocolate chips, a weakness of Gunner's, who ate like a third.

"What about your wolf, though? I don't have any cans of dog food. But I might have a can of Spam in the cupboard."

"As if I'd eat that."

Her phone rang and she grimaced as she saw Howard's number. Although to be fair, she had no reason to be annoyed with him. He'd actually done something kind today by bringing Kylie over even if Gunner goaded him into doing it. Still, perhaps this was the beginning of a less hostile style of co-parenting, which would be the best present she could have asked for.

Could be it was Annabelle calling.

She waggled her phone. "Can you not bark for a second while I talk to Squishy?"

"Ha. Ha. So funny."

She answered. "Hello."

"Kylie!" Howard gasped her name.

"Howard? Is something wrong?" They'd left not that long ago, and while the roads were clear, they would be slippery.

"There was an accident."

A statement that caused her heart to stop. "Oh my god. Annabelle, is she okay?"

"No, they took her," Howard sobbed.

"Who took her? Is she in an ambulance?"

"No. I paid my debt. I don't understand. Why would they take her?"

Her blood ran cold.

Gunner snatched the phone and hit speaker. "Keeler, tell me exactly where you are."

"On the road. About a mile from my parents' place." His voice lowered. "You gotta help me find her. They took her! She's just a little girl. Why would they do that? I gave them everything they asked for plus some to leave me alone."

"Stay with your car. I'm on my way."

Gunner handed Kylie back the phone and headed for the door with her on his heels.

"Stay here," he advised as he shoved his feet into his boots.

"No."

"If Howard's talking about those thugs, then it's going to be dangerous." He didn't sugarcoat it.

"I don't care." She broke as she said, "They took my Squishy!"

"They will regret that." A grim promise. "I will get her back."

Kylie couldn't speak. Her throat was too tight with emotion. She piled on her coat and grabbed a hat and mitts just in case before slipping on her boots and following him outside. A light snow had begun to fall again.

Who kidnapped my baby? It had to be the people Howard owed the gambling money to. She had to be so scared.

Kylie wrung her hands as he sped to the location Howard indicated on the phone. He turned out to be easy to find, his car half in a ditch, the driver side showing a massive dent from impact. The car that hit it was a few yards ahead of it, doors open, the hood crunched.

Howard stood beside his wreck, shoulders hunched, head down.

The moment they exited the car, Howard went for Gunner, blabbering a mile a minute. "They must have been waiting. They shot out of a side road"—Howard pointed—"and clipped my front end. The air bags went off when we hit the ditch. Before I could get out, they had grabbed Annabelle from the back seat."

"Who?" Gunner asked.

"Same ones who went to see Kylie the other day."

Kylie went ballistic. "This is your fault!"

"I know," Howard admitted on a broken note. "I thought paying them would be enough, but they said something about settling an old score. A daughter for a brother, which made no sense."

Judging by Gunner's pinched lips, it did. It hit Kylie a second later. "This is about that woman you thought might be out for revenge."

Rather than reply, Gunner started stripping.

Her mouth rounded, but it was Howard who sputtered, "What the fuck are you doing?"

"Going to find Annabelle," he said as his shirt came off, revealing his muscled chest.

His hands went to his pants, and Kylie recovered enough to say, "Now is not the time for your delusions. We need to call the police." Which Kylie should have done the moment Howard called her.

"The police will never find them." Stated as Gunner shoved down his pants.

Howard exclaimed, "Kylie, what the fuck?"

And then it was her turn to murmur, "What the fuck?" as her lover started to change.

Into a wolf.

16

THERE WAS no easy or gentle way to shift, not when time might be of essence. While Gunner didn't like the fact Howard watched with a dropped jaw, he was more concerned with Kylie.

She stared with rounded eyes. He stared back for a second.

Howard exclaimed, "You're dating a fucking werewolf!"

Yeah, she was, and Keeler had better watch that tone, or Gunner would eat his face. Later. After he found Annabelle. He could smell her and those who'd abducted her. They probably planned to snatch the kid and use their car, only they'd hit too hard and the front passenger wheel didn't survive the impact.

He lifted his head to track the direction they'd

taken. No real surprise, they'd entered the woods. What he didn't like? It wasn't just the two thugs he'd beaten before. He smelled a third, the putrid aroma chilling as it indicated a monster such as the ones he'd thought destroyed when they took out Sascha in London.

Joella must have recruited it, and he could only thank the lucky North Star that she'd not sent it after them earlier. The monsters were hard to kill, not feeling pain, healing quickly, and bloodthirsty. He'd have to be careful. The light falling snow hampered his tracking somewhat, with it filling in the tracks left behind as well as diminishing visibility. But his nose kept on the scent, leading him through the woods in a straight line so he could only assume they had a destination nearby.

The trail led him to a snowy, unpaved gravel driveway. While knowing they probably watched, Gunner still trotted up the drive, alert for movement and sound.

While he paid attention to the front, the wind blowing past him camouflaged the threat at his back. The beast attacked, and he barely had time to brace when it hit him. The hairy wolf monster with its batlike features hissed as it sought to grab hold and tear.

Gunner wiggled and twisted, snapping his teeth.

The beast recoiled and snarled. Gunner was at a disadvantage, the wolfman monster having clawed hands that could grasp. However, its single-mindedness proved to be its downfall. It was so intent on trying to rip out Gunner's throat, it didn't notice Gunner positioning himself so his hind legs could dig into its soft underbelly, his own claws flexing and pricking flesh. Not enough to disembowel, but the creature retained enough wits to realize it needed to back off and regroup.

As if he'd allow that. Gunner pounced, not aiming for the head or neck as it expected, but the legs, his powerful jaws clamping around its ankle and shin, biting hard enough it snapped. Even its ability to ignore pain couldn't keep the monster upright. It hit the ground, and Gunner pounced, not wasting time doing the same to an arm, breaking it like a twig.

Its neck was next, crushed until the beast went limp.

Gunner spat out the hair and blood, wiping his muzzle in the snow and leaving it red. One monster down, and he didn't know if there were more. He hoped not.

He continued up the driveway, spotting lights in the distance, a faint glow amidst the thickly falling snow. The path ended in a massive clearing holding a house still under construction, the outside covered in that plastic they put on before the siding. The windows and doors were in place, annoying since he had paws, not hands.

But he'd wager Joella expected him, seeing as how the main entrance suddenly swung open.

A trap? Most definitely, but Annabelle's scent went inside, meaning he had no choice.

He stepped slowly inside, eyes straight but senses wide. A guy on each side of the entrance, their scent that of strangers. He didn't smell gun oil, but that didn't mean they were weapon free.

Most likely they'd been told to hold off on attacking, given Joella sat on an uninstalled kitchen cabinet, grinning. Not so the kid huddled below her feet.

"You're here quicker than expected. I knew you'd come for the girl."

A girl who showed spirit in the glare she aimed at her kidnapper. Flanking Joella, the bruised and battered thugs who'd chosen to ignore his warning. They wouldn't get a second one.

He bared his teeth. The smaller thug with the face tattoos pulled a switchblade. Dumbass. He'd better hope he had good and fast aim because Gunner wouldn't be playing. Given he was outnumbered, he'd have to be precise and deadly.

He uttered a low growl.

Joella tapped her chin. "I do believe you're asking me to let the girl go. But I'm thinking she'll be useful for keeping you in line while I administer the last of my brother's research." She snapped her fingers, and the big thug with his broken and taped nose lifted a solid black case. He opened it to reveal five vials filled with a noxious-appearing cloudy liquid.

It turned Gunner's stomach to see it, as he knew what it could do. The monster he'd killed being a prime example.

"This was the last batch he ever made, and with his notes gone because of you and your friends, we'll never be able to replicate his brilliance. But I'm not one to let things go to waste, and I thought why not give it to someone worthy of it, like the person who had a hand in his death?"

He'd actually only been a spectator when Brock tore Sascha apart. However, Brock proved to be immune to Sascha's experiment.

It should be known Gunner would have been willing to let her inject him if he thought Annabelle would be safely released. However, Joella's depravity meant she couldn't be trusted. She wouldn't hesitate to hurt or kill a kid.

Which meant he had to act. Four guys and

Joella, plus a sweet girl he didn't want to traumatize meant he had to be tricky. He stared at Annabelle, wishing he could tell her to not be scared. To hide until it was over.

She cocked her head and then glanced at Joella to say, "Why do you keep talking to the wolf like he's a person?"

"Because he is. This is your mommy's boyfriend, Gunner. Surprise, he's a werewolf."

Annabelle gaped in his direction. "Gunner? Is that you?"

He bobbed his head, unsure if knowing the truth would frighten her more or not.

She smiled. "I knew my hero would come for me."

The claim had Joella cackling. "Your hero is about to receive his just rewards."

"Wrong. You are." Annabelle popped to her feet and bolted so quickly no one moved at first.

But then, when the men did start to follow, Joella screamed, "You idiots, she's just trying to distract you."

And she'd done a fine job. The guy to his left pivoted away from Gunner so Gunner took him out first, lunging and biting down on his thigh. The hot spurt of blood indicated he'd hit an artery. Bull's-eye.

He let go knowing it wouldn't be long before the guy was down for the count. His buddy on the other side started moving in his direction when Gunner whipped his head around and snarled.

It stopped the fellow in his tracks, but only for a second, as Joella yelled, "You idiot, use the taser."

The fellow jerked his arm forward, the device in his hand barely aimed before he activated it. Gunner jerked to the side, and the electrodes missed. He didn't.

The guy screamed and held his crushed hand to his chest. Since the noise bothered Gunner, he could only imagine how it affected Annabelle. His next move, which involved slamming into the guy, smacked the thug's head hard enough he passed out. Or died. Didn't really matter. He went after the guy with the briefcase next. That formula couldn't be allowed to survive.

The unlatched case got tossed at him. Two of the vials slipped out onto the floor but didn't break. He ignored them to snarl in the big man's direction.

The man muttered, "Fuck this," and ran through an unfinished archway to another room. Not the same one as Annabelle.

Speaking of whom, he should check on her, seeing as how Joella had also disappeared. But not so the tattooed guy. He held out his knife as if he really thought it would help.

"Come on, doggy. I'm going to make myself a coat out of your fur."

Gunner snorted.

The fellow ran at him, screaming. Gunner stepped aside at the last moment, whirled, and threw himself at Tattoo's legs. Tattoo went down and didn't move. Mostly likely because of the spreading pool of blood under him. Stabbed himself when he fell. An ignoble death for an ignoble asshole.

Which left only Joella. He went in the direction Annabelle had gone and found both scents. No surprise, Joella went after the kid in hopes of using her as a hostage.

Only Annabelle wasn't having it. She held a nail gun and aimed it at Joella, her voice quavering as she said, "Stop or else."

"Brat!" Joella reached, and Annabelle fired.

The nail hit, but it wasn't enough to deter Joella. She grabbed the kid, who squirmed and fought.

Not for long. Gunner came to the snarling rescue, only to pull back as Joella whirled, holding Annabelle in a headlock, her eyes wild with madness and desperation.

"Touch me and I will snap her neck."

He didn't doubt she would.

Joella stepped sideways, dragging Annabelle with her. Just as she took another, with a smirk on her lips, the kid acted, angling her head enough to bite the arm holding her.

Joella screeched. Annabelle broke free and ran behind Gunner, who had a clear line to Joella. One leap and he'd be crunching her throat, ending her reign of terror.

Joella's lips stretched into a grotesque smile. "Go ahead, tear into me in front of the girl. Let her see what a monster you are."

He hesitated.

Mocking laughter emerged from Joella. "Weak. So weak. And you wonder why Sascha wanted to improve upon your kind."

He retreated a step. Joella's lips twisted in triumph, and then Annabelle spat the one thing he couldn't ignore.

"If you don't get rid of her now, you know she's gonna come back later. What if she hurts Mommy?"

He glanced at Annabelle.

She stared right back and said softly, "Remember what we talked about when it comes to bad guys."

Never hesitate to kill.

He could only hope she looked away as he

pounced. Joella didn't have a chance to scream as he tore into her neck, ending her reign of terror.

And in the process starting a new one with a kid who would be traumatized for life.

He ducked his head, conscious of the blood in his fur.

A pale Annabelle didn't run screaming, though. She neared and put a hand on his fur murmuring, "My hero."

He side-eyed Annabelle and found her grinning. "How cool is that? My mom is dating a werewolf."

Fuck. He'd better explain to her how this was like the biggest of secrets because if the Cabal found out... Surely they wouldn't hurt a kid? What of Kylie? They'd better not try anything, or they'd find out just how rabid he could be.

"We should go find Daddy and Mommy. They're probably worried."

Understatement of the year.

He led her from the scene of violence to the road rather than the woods. The driveway must have been the spot the car had emerged from before crashing into Howard's sedan. Annabelle kept her hand buried in his fur, as if afraid to lose him. He couldn't reassure her that would never happen despite the thickly falling snow.

The kid had balls of steel. She didn't tremble in fear, like most who encountered a wolf. She also didn't seem to care he couldn't reply as she talked. "So have you been always been a werewolf? In this book I read, the boy was born that way. But in a show I watch, the man was bitten."

He glanced over at her, lifted a lip to show teeth and hoped it didn't send her screaming.

The kid laughed. "Bitten. Wow. That's so wild."

She was wild. Who knew a young person could be so brave?

She kept chattering as they neared the edge of the driveway and stepped onto the road about two hundred yards from the vehicles. The snow swirled and danced across the pavement, revealing and obscuring the site of the crash long enough a watching Kylie spilled from the truck, yelling, "Squishy, thank god you're safe."

"Gunner saved me!"

Kylie's gaze then moved to him. Her eyes widened in shock, most likely because of the blood still coating his muzzle. He'd tried to wipe it in the snow, but nothing short of a shower would get the stickiness off.

While Kylie might be speechless, Howard wasn't. "Get away from that monster!"

Kylie's mouth opened as if she'd speak, only to hesitate.

Before she could reject him, Gunner slipped from Annabelle's grasp and fled to the woods.

Where a wild animal like him belonged.

Alone.

17

Kylie was still processing her shock at seeing Annabelle emerge from the forest with a wolf that it took her a moment.

A moment to realize that was blood on the fur.

A moment to realize familiar eyes were gauging her reaction.

A moment too long. He whirled around and disappeared from sight.

"Gunner! Come back!" Annabelle cried out, but when she would have run after him into the woods, Howard swept in and scooped her.

"Thank God you're safe. I was so worried," he murmured.

Kylie joined them, stroking a hand over Annabelle's cheek, the skin wet. Teary eyes met hers.

"Mommy, you have to find him."

Find him how? The fast-falling snow already obscured his tracks.

"Let him go. I knew there was something off about that guy." Howard scowled in the direction of the woods.

Annabelle shoved out of his hug. "Gunner saved me."

"He's a killer. A monster," Howard stated.

In some respects, he was right, but… She glanced at her baby. "He rescued our daughter."

"From people who were after him," Howard replied. "Sounds like this is his problem."

"Says the man who caused us to be threatened when he was in trouble," Kylie hotly retorted. "Or have you conveniently forgotten Gunner bailed you out?"

His eyes widened. "He told you!"

"He did because he valued our safety more than the horrible promise you tried to make him keep. How could you, Howard? Putting our child in danger because you wanted to gamble?" She went after him and might have really torn him a new one if Annabelle didn't suddenly say, "Someone's coming."

Headlights in the swirling snow turned into a blacked-out Suburban, the type cops liked to use. The unmarked vehicle parked behind the truck but didn't turn on any kind of flashing lights.

Please, not the police. She had no idea what she'd say.

People emerged, two men and two women.

The guy with a brush cut stared at her and said, "You must be Kylie, Gunner's fiancée."

"We're not engaged," was her dumb reply.

A gorgeous woman with her long hair pulled back strode to the edge of the woods. "I smell blood and wolf." She turned an uncanny gaze on Kylie. "Where's Gunner?"

"Who are you?" she asked instead.

"Friends," the brush-cut guy replied. "I'm Brock. This is Quinn and Dr. Silver. And that woman stalking into the woods is my pain-in-the-ass princess. Arianna, do not go in there without me," he bellowed.

In reply, Arianna showed him a middle finger.

Howard's head whipped back and forth as he took them in before he muttered, "Why do I get the impression Gunner's friends are just like him?"

Quinn smirked. "Fuck me, I hope not. He's an ornery bastard."

A shocked Kylie exhaled, "Language, there's a child!"

"Are you sure she's Gunner's mate?" murmured the doctor as she grabbed a bag from the truck.

"Can we save the small talk for later?" Brock interjected. "What happened? Where's Gunner?"

Annabelle pointed to the forest. "He saved me from the bad guys and brought me back to my parents. But then he ran off."

"He was covered in blood," Kylie added. "I don't know if it was his."

"Most of it was from the bad guys," Annabelle stated with some pride.

Howard winced.

"Stupid fucker was supposed to wait for us before going after Joella," Brock muttered. "Good thing I was tracking his phone, or we'd have never found you."

Kylie lifted her chin. "My daughter was kidnapped. He didn't want to wait to rescue her."

"Always playing the hero." Brock shook his head. "Guess we'd better go drag his ass out before he goes into another ten-year funk."

Hearing his friend say it aloud made her realize Gunner had not been kidding about his mental state. A state caused by her because he thought she wouldn't accept him.

Wouldn't be able to accept a werewolf as her husband.

Could she?

She glanced at her daughter, who said softly, "We need to find him, Mommy. He looked so sad."

Howard interjected. "The only place you're going is home."

"I want to help!" huffed Annabelle.

"Why don't you get some hot cocoa and snacks ready? I'll bet he's going to be hungry." Kylie offered a soothing alternative.

"You can't seriously think I'm going to let him near our daughter," Howard exclaimed.

Her daughter crossed her arms, lower lip jutting. "Gunner's a hero."

"Indeed, he is, sweetheart," Quinn stated. "How about you tell me all about it back at your mom's place. I'm sure your mom would appreciate my wife having a peek at you to make sure you're all good."

"We're supposed to be having dinner with my parents," Howard protested.

Brock leaned close and hissed, "You will go with Quinn, and you will behave, or so help me fucking Christ, I will forget it's Christmas and tear out your tongue."

Howard blinked. Nodded.

As they clambered into the suburban, Brock glanced at Kylie. "You going with them?"

It was tempting to leave this stormy road for the familiarity and safety of her home. But Gunner was out in those woods, alone and hurting. "I'm coming with you."

The woods were quiet except for her. She huffed. She crunched snow. Unlike the man ghosting ahead of her. At times she thought she'd lost him, and fear had her sucking in a harsh breath. Then Brock would appear by her side and point.

He followed a path only he could see, and it occurred to her she trusted him with her life because no way she could have found her way back, not with the darkness and falling snow.

When they emerged into an area cleared of trees in which sat an unfinished house, she stumbled. It didn't take a wild guess to realize this was where Annabelle had been taken. The wide-open front door made that clear. Arianna stood outside, waiting for them.

Her teeth gleamed as she said, "About time you caught up."

"Says the princess who escaped the drama."

Arianna's nose wrinkled. "I heard enough." And then in a cryptic aside to Kylie added, "Don't worry. I'll make sure he doesn't remember and make your life hell. The kid, too, if you'd like."

Before Kylie could ask what she meant, Arianna slipped into the building.

As for Kylie, she stepped more slowly, not sure she wanted to see inside.

Brock noticed her hesitation. "You might not want to go in."

Turned out, she didn't have to.

A wolf appeared in the open doorway. He took one look at her and howled.

To her surprise, Brock snapped, "Don't you start with that."

The wolf gave him a reproachful look.

"Did it ever occur to you that she's here with me and Princess because she wants to be? Because she cares about you?" Brock gestured.

The wolf glanced at her then away.

She took a step closer and murmured softly, "I'm sorry about earlier, Gunner. I didn't mean to make you feel bad. This whole situation is a little strange."

Arianna snorted as she emerged. "Wait until you find out what I am."

"Not now, princess. Can't you see they're having a moment?" Brock shushed her.

Kylie was curious to know what she meant, but that could happen later. Once she'd fixed things with Gunner.

A few more paces brought her close enough she could have reached out and touched him. She kept her hands clasped as she said, "Guess you were telling the truth about the werewolf thing."

He snorted.

"Does this mean we'll need to build a doghouse in the backyard?"

Brock barked with laughter. "Please do and make him use it every time he's a dumbass."

"Now, puppy, that's not nice. Given Gunner's just like you, he'd be in it all the time," Arianna drawled.

"Hey!" Brock protested.

"Let's leave them alone to talk, and I'll show you what we have to deal with inside." Arianna shoved him, and while she might be petite, she managed to send Brock stumbling and grumbling, "Bossy woman. It's like you purposely turn me on at the worst possible time."

They disappeared into the house, leaving Kylie alone with the wolf.

A wolf who would never hurt her.

"May I?" She held out her hand and waited for his nod before stripping her glove and running her fingers through his hair.

Coarse but not insanely so. Frosted on the outer layer but, as her fingers sank to the deeper fur, warm.

She crouched to bring herself more eye level,

murmuring, "I'm sorry you thought I wouldn't accept this part of you."

He huffed hotly.

"Guess you're not delusional after all."

He wheezed as if laughing.

"I am still not crazy about the whole killing thing," she stated. "But in this case, I am glad you made sure the people who tried to hurt my baby won't ever be able to again."

His low growl brought a small chuckle.

"Guess I never have to worry about anyone messing with us."

His head bobbed.

"In case it wasn't clear, this is me asking you to stay."

He pawed the ground.

"I'll assume that's a yes."

He almost knocked her over as his whole body wiggled in excitement.

The sweeping tail had Brock, who'd just rejoined them with Arianna, exclaiming, "Jeezus, bro, put that thing away before you knock someone out."

Gunner yipped.

"Good boy." Brock went to pat him, and Gunner bared teeth. The other man laughed, not bothered at all. "Nice to see you haven't lost the attitude. How about losing the fur, though? Pretty sure your little lady would prefer it if you could give her a real kiss instead of trying to sniff her crotch."

"He told me he might not be able to return to his man shape until morning."

"Bah. That's because he's just a plain ol' Lycan. Good thing he's got me to straighten him out." Brock grabbed hold of his head and stared long and hard before uttering in a low rumble, "Change."

It sounded dumb. Yet it worked. Before her disbelieving eyes, the fur receded, the limbs reshaped, until a very naked and shivering Gunner stood there.

She threw herself at him for a proper hug, but when she would have kissed him, he turned his face. "Might want to wait until I brush my teeth."

"Fuck me, I should have probably waited to do that back at the truck so you could have some pants." Brock added, "I don't need my princess admiring some other bloke's wanker."

"Please. Everyone knows cocks aren't what women admire. It's all about their great big—" Arianna looked at Kylie and winked before she said, "Hearts."

Brock protested. "Are you calling me soft?"

A shivering Gunner still managed to quip, "Bro, I saw your cardigans in the closet at your seaside cottage."

"Because it gets brisk," Brock explained.

"With elbow patches," added Gunner with a smirk.

"I'm rough on clothes."

"Speaking of which, mine are back at the truck," Gunner remarked.

Kylie eyed his feet. "You'll lose some toes if you walk barefoot back to the road."

"I can carry him," Brock offered with a smirk.

In the end, Brock jogged down the driveway to fetch the clothes, while she sat in the house with Gunner, ignoring the blood stains on the floor. At least there were no bodies visible, and she didn't go looking to find them.

Gunner held her hand and stroked it. "Sorry the day ended up such a clusterfuck."

"You're alive, Annabelle is safe. I'd say things could have been worse."

"I should have done a better job protecting you."

"I'm going to assume this Joella person that was behind it won't be bothering us anymore?"

He shook his head.

"Any other enemies I need to worry about?"

Another negative.

"Don't be so sure. Howard was pretty freaked," she noted with a grimace as Arianna returned from another room in the house.

"Your ex won't be a problem once I'm done with him," the other woman stated.

"You can't kill him! He's Annabelle's dad."

"Fear not. I'm just going to make him forget a few things, and maybe tweak his attitude a little bit."

Kylie frowned. "I don't understand."

"May I tell her?" Gunner asked.

"And ruin my fun?" Arianna taunted. She smiled. Wide. Fangs dropped.

"Oh my god, you're a vampire?" Kylie squeaked.

"In the flesh. And before you freak, no, I won't suck your blood. I have Brock for that. I will, however, mesmerize your ex into thinking he had a car accident. No werewolves, no kidnapping. Nothing except a lovely rescue by his ex-wife and her new boyfriend. Sound good?"

Kylie nodded. And then more tentatively, "You won't make me forget, will you?"

"That's up to you and Gunner."

"I'm good, but Annabelle..." She chewed her lower lip.

Gunner put his hand over hers. "Is a tough kid. But you're her mom. It's up to you."

"Will it hurt her to forget?"

Arianna snorted. "No, but are you sure you want to do that? I mean, how cool is it for her to have a step-daddy who fights bad guys and turns into a wolf?"

Kylie couldn't help but grin. "Knowing my kid? It's probably the most epic thing ever." Her expression sobered. "I'm more worried about the kidnapping and violence she experienced, though."

"Don't decide right away. Talk it over with her first," Arianna suggested.

A rumbling engine turned into the truck plowing up the driveway in four-wheel drive. In short order, Gunner wore his clothes, and they sat in the truck, waiting.

Kylie wondered why until Brock and Arianna emerged. Each held a makeshift torch made of wood wrapped in a burning rag, which they shook out and tossed through the open door from which smoke trickled.

"They're burning the place?"

"Best way to hide the evidence." Gunner's soft reply.

"But the people who died..." Whose bodies had to be inside. "Won't forensics still be able to tell how they died?"

"Not if they set the stage correctly. Keep in mind, our kind have been hiding our tracks for centuries."

"What about the cars on the road?"

"Don't worry. I'm sure Brock and Arianna have a plan."

A plan that hadn't taken into account the three-seater truck. The pair took one look at the bench front seat, and Brock grinned. "Guess you're riding in my lap, princess."

"I thought dogs liked to be in the back, jowls in the wind." Arianna jerked her thumb at the box.

Kylie leaned close to whisper, "Do they always fight like that?"

"I think it's foreplay for them," was Gunner's amused reply.

Her nose wrinkled. "I prefer our version better."

Gunner chuckled. "So do I, Lily."

The ride to the house proved crowded, the wide Brock squishing her into Gunner. Arianna did end up in his lap but didn't seem to mind.

The roads were getting ugly by the time they reached her house. It looked warm and cozy with its Christmas lights guiding their way.

Annabelle flew out the door the moment they pulled in. Gunner slid out first and helped Kylie next. He'd not had a chance to let go when they were squished in a hug.

"You're home!"

"As if there was any doubt." Arianna sniffed as she passed them. "Is that hot cocoa I smell?"

"Yes. And pizza. Quinn ordered like five of them."

And that was how their Christmas ended, with them crammed into her living room, eating pizza off napkins. Everyone safe and sound.

A mellow Howard spent the night on the couch since the storm made it impossible for him to get home. Of course, that calmness only happened once Arianna was done with him. His first words upon seeing Gunner were, "Stay away from me and my daughter. You and your crooked friends."

Kylie felt no guilt at all that his memory of the night changed after Arianna did her thing. To his recollection, his car stalled in the storm, and he'd been picked up by Kylie and Gunner. Little did he know that that someone smashed into his car after he abandoned it. Those same people fled the scene and somehow started a fire in an unfinished home, where they perished.

As for Annabelle... Kylie took her aside to have a chat.

"I know tonight must have been scary."

Squishy's expression turned bright. "It was, but I knew Gunner would save me."

"Still, that kind of violence—"

"Was gross, but he didn't have a choice, Mommy."

"There is a way to make you forget," she offered.

"Like Arianna did with Daddy?" Annabelle had been paying attention.

"Yes."

"No, thank you."

Kylie wanted to argue, but at the same time, she wanted to respect Annabelle's wishes. But she reserved the right to act if her child showed any signs of trauma.

Given the late hour and storm, it wasn't just Howard who stayed over.

Arianna and Brock took the basement, which Kylie protested as being the least comfortable spot, but they insisted. Given the vampire thing, it did make sense, though.

Quinn and the doctor took her old bedroom, despite being offered the master.

As the house settled for the night, she and Gunner spooned. A remarkably mundane ending to a high-strung day.

Despite it all, she whispered, "Thanks for giving me the best Christmas."

He stiffened. "How do you figure?"

"Because you finally came back to me."

And that was all she ever wanted.

EPILOGUE

A YEAR LATER...

THE CHRISTMAS LIGHTS on the house weren't quite *Christmas Vacation* crazy but close. And Kylie loved it.

Gunner had done a bunch of work on the house since he'd moved in, from repainting the siding to redoing the porches, even fixing the landscaping. His efforts were noticed by the neighbors, resulting in him taking on handyman jobs with strict hours that had him home by dinner and off on weekends. Because, as he said, he'd already missed enough time making memories.

Christmas morning came in the form of a squeal. "Mommy! Gus!" The name Annabelle adopted for her stepdad who'd made Kylie an honest woman that summer in a private ceremony attended only by his army friends, their wives, a mellow Howard, and Annabelle.

Kylie headed downstairs with her husband, smiling as her daughter giggled from the living room.

"I wonder what's got her so excited?" she murmured. Squishy usually wasn't one to open gifts without Kylie.

"You'll see," was Gunner's mysterious reply.

They entered to see Annabelle hugging a puppy.

Kylie's eyes rounded because it looked like a wolf. She glanced at Gunner, who shrugged and winked. "Every kid should have a pet growing up."

Which probably explained her present. An orange kitten which Annabelle presented after lunch when she and Gunner ran out to run a supposed errand.

As she stroked the soft, purring body, Gunner put his arm around her. "I know it's not a replacement for the kids you wanted."

She glanced at him and smiled. "I already have a perfect kid and the man I always wanted."

They both got the happily ever after they deserved and the first of many howling great Noels.

NEED MORE FURRY ROMANCE? FOR MORE BOOKS AND FUN SEE EVELANGLAIS.COM

www.ingramcontent.com/pod-product-compliance
Lightning Source LLC
LaVergne TN
LVHW031540060526
838200LV00056B/4578